60

FARRAR
STRAUS
GIROUX

BOOKS BY FLANNERY O'CONNOR

NOVELS

Wise Blood

The Violent Bear It Away

STORIES

A Good Man Is Hard to Find

Everything That Rises Must Converge
with an introduction by Robert Fitzgerald

The Complete Stories of Flannery O'Connor
edited and with an introduction
by Robert Giroux

NON-FICTION

Mystery and Manners
edited and with an introduction
by Robert and Sally Fitzgerald

The Habit of Being
edited and with an introduction
by Sally Fitzgerald

WISE BLOOD

WISE
BLOOD

FLANNERY O'CONNOR

Farrar, Straus and Giroux

New York

Farrar, Straus and Giroux
19 Union Square West, New York 10003

Library of Congress Control Number: 2006937221
Paperback ISBN-13: 978-0-374-53063-1
Paperback ISBN-10: 0-374-53063-7

www.fsgbooks.com

1 2 3 4 5 6 7 8 9 10

For Regina

AUTHOR'S NOTE
TO THE SECOND EDITION

WISE BLOOD has reached the age of ten and is still alive. My critical powers are just sufficient to determine this, and I am gratified to be able to say it. The book was written with zest and, if possible, it should be read that way. It is a comic novel about a Christian *malgré lui*, and as such, very serious, for all comic novels that are any good must be about matters of life and death. *Wise Blood* was written by an author congenitally innocent of theory, but one with certain preoccupations. That belief in Christ is to some a matter of life and death has been a stumbling block for readers who would prefer to think it a matter of no great consequence. For them Hazel Motes' integrity lies in his trying with such vigor to get rid of the ragged figure who moves from tree to tree in the back of his mind. For the author Hazel's integrity lies in his not being able to. Does one's integrity ever lie in what he is not able to do? I think that usually it does, for free will does not mean one will, but many wills conflicting in one man. Freedom cannot be conceived simply. It is a mystery and one which a novel, even a comic novel, can only be asked to deepen.

—1962

CHAPTER 1

Hazel Motes sat at a forward angle on the green plush train seat, looking one minute at the window as if he might want to jump out of it, and the next down the aisle at the other end of the car. The train was racing through tree tops that fell away at intervals and showed the sun standing, very red, on the edge of the farthest woods. Nearer, the plowed fields curved and faded and the few hogs nosing in the furrows looked like large spotted stones. Mrs. Wally Bee Hitchcock, who was facing Motes in the section, said that she thought the early evening like this was the prettiest time of day and she asked him if he didn't think so too. She was a fat woman with pink collars and cuffs and pear-shaped legs that slanted off the train seat and didn't reach the floor.

He looked at her a second and, without answering, leaned forward and stared down the length of the car again. She turned to see what was back there but all she saw was a child peering around one of the sections and, farther up at

3

the end of the car, the porter opening the closet where the sheets were kept.

"I guess you're going home," she said, turning back to him again. He didn't look, to her, much over twenty, but he had a stiff black broad-brimmed hat on his lap, a hat that an elderly country preacher would wear. His suit was a glaring blue and the price tag was still stapled on the sleeve of it.

He didn't answer her or move his eyes from whatever he was looking at. The sack at his feet was an army duffel bag and she decided that he had been in the army and had been released and that now he was going home. She wanted to get close enough to see what the suit had cost him but she found herself squinting instead at his eyes, trying almost to look into them. They were the color of pecan shells and set in deep sockets. The outline of a skull under his skin was plain and insistent.

She felt irked and wrenched her attention loose and squinted at the price tag. The suit had cost him $11.98. She felt that that placed him and looked at his face again as if she were fortified against it now. He had a nose like a shrike's bill and a long vertical crease on either side of his mouth; his hair looked as if it had been permanently flattened under the heavy hat, but his eyes were what held her attention longest. Their settings were so deep that they seemed, to her, almost like passages leading somewhere and she leaned halfway across the space that separated the

4

two seats, trying to see into them. He turned toward the window suddenly and then almost as quickly turned back again to where his stare had been fixed.

What he was looking at was the porter. When he had first got on the train, the porter had been standing between the two cars—a thick-figured man with a round yellow bald head. Haze had stopped and the porter's eyes had turned toward him and away, indicating which car he was to go into. When he didn't go, the porter said, "To the left," irritably, "to the left," and Haze had moved on.

"Well," Mrs. Hitchcock said, "there's no place like home."

He gave her a glance and saw the flat of her face, reddish under a cap of fox-colored hair. She had got on two stops back. He had never seen her before that. "I got to go see the porter," he said. He got up and went toward the end of the car where the porter had begun making up a berth. He stopped beside him and leaned on a seat arm, but the porter didn't look at him. He was pulling a wall of the section farther out.

"How long does it take you to make one up?"

"Seven minutes," the porter said, not looking at him.

Haze sat down on the seat arm. He said, "I'm from Eastrod."

"That isn't on this line," the porter said. "You on the wrong train."

5

"Going to the city," Haze said. "I said I was raised in Eastrod."

The porter didn't say anything.

"Eastrod," Haze said, louder.

The porter jerked the shade down. "You want your berth made up now, or what you standing there for?" he asked.

"Eastrod," Haze said. "Near Melsy."

The porter wrenched one side of the seat flat. "I'm from Chicago," he said. He wrenched the other side down. When he bent over, the back of his neck came out in three bulges.

"Yeah, I bet you are," Haze said with a leer.

"Your feet in the middle of the aisle. Somebody going to want to get by you," the porter said, turning suddenly and brushing past.

Haze got up and hung there a few seconds. He looked as if he were held by a rope caught in the middle of his back and attached to the train ceiling. He watched the porter move in a fine controlled lurch down the aisle and disappear at the other end of the car. He knew him to be a Parrum nigger from Eastrod. He went back to his section and folded into a slouched position and settled one foot on a pipe that ran under the window. Eastrod filled his head and then went out beyond and filled the space that stretched from the train across the empty darkening fields. He saw the two houses and the rust-colored road and the few Negro shacks and the one barn and the stall with the red and white CCC snuff ad peeling across the side of it.

"Are you going home?" Mrs. Hitchcock asked.

He looked at her sourly and gripped the black hat by the brim. "No, I ain't," he said in a sharp high nasal Tennessee voice.

Mrs. Hitchcock said neither was she. She told him she had been a Miss Weatherman before she married and that she was going to Florida to visit her married daughter, Sarah Lucile. She said it seemed like she had never had time to take a trip that far off. The way things happened, one thing after another, it seemed like time went by so fast you couldn't tell if you were young or old.

He thought he could tell her she was old if she asked him. He stopped listening to her after a while. The porter passed back up the aisle and didn't look at him. Mrs. Hitchcock lost her train of talk. "I guess you're on your way to visit somebody?" she asked.

"Going to Taulkinham," he said and ground himself into the seat and looked at the window. "Don't know nobody there, but I'm going to do some things.

"I'm going to do some things I never have done before," he said and gave her a sidelong glance and curled his mouth slightly.

She said she knew an Albert Sparks from Taulkinham. She said he was her sister-in-law's brother-in-law and that he . . .

"I ain't from Taulkinham," he said. "I said I'm going

there, that's all." Mrs. Hitchcock began to talk again but he cut her short and said, "That porter was raised in the same place where I was raised but he says he's from Chicago."

Mrs. Hitchcock said she knew a man who lived in Chi . . .

"You might as well go one place as another," he said. "That's all I know."

Mrs. Hitchcock said well that time flies. She said she hadn't seen her sister's children in five years and she didn't know if she'd know them if she saw them. There were three of them, Roy, Bubber, and John Wesley. John Wesley was six years old and he had written her a letter, dear Mammadoll. They called her Mammadoll and her husband Papadoll . . .

"I reckon you think you been redeemed," he said.

Mrs. Hitchcock snatched at her collar.

"I reckon you think you been redeemed," he repeated.

She blushed. After a second she said yes, life was an inspiration and then she said she was hungry and asked him if he didn't want to go into the diner. He put on the fierce black hat and followed her out of the car.

The dining car was full and people were waiting to get in it. He and Mrs. Hitchcock stood in line for a half-hour, rocking in the narrow passageway and every few minutes flattening themselves against the side to let a trickle of people through. Mrs. Hitchcock talked to the woman on the side of her. Hazel Motes looked at the wall. Mrs. Hitchcock told the woman about her sister's husband who was with the City Water Works in Toolafalls, Alabama, and the lady told about a cousin who had cancer of the throat. Finally they got almost up to the entrance of the diner and could see inside it. There was a steward beckoning people to places and handing out menus. He was a white man with greased black hair and a greased black look to his suit. He moved like a crow, darting from table to table. He motioned for two people and the line moved up so that Haze and Mrs. Hitchcock and the lady she was talking to were ready to go next. In a minute two more people left. The steward beckoned and Mrs. Hitchcock and the woman walked in and Haze followed them. The man stopped him and said, "Only two," and pushed him back to the doorway.

Haze's face turned an ugly red. He tried to get behind the next person and then he tried to get through the line to go back to the car he had come from but there were too many people bunched in the opening. He had to stand there while everyone around looked at him. No one left for a while. Finally a woman at the far end of the car got up and the steward jerked his hand. Haze hesitated and saw the hand jerk again. He lurched up the aisle, falling against two tables on the way and getting his hand wet in somebody's coffee. The steward placed him with three youngish women dressed like parrots.

Their hands were resting on the table, red-speared at

the tips. He sat down and wiped his hand on the table-cloth. He didn't take off his hat. The women had finished eating and were smoking cigarettes. They stopped talking when he sat down. He pointed to the first thing on the menu and the steward, standing over him, said, "Write it down, sonny," and winked at one of the women; she made a noise in her nose. He wrote it down and the steward went away with it. He sat and looked in front of him, glum and intense, at the neck of the woman across from him. At intervals her hand holding the cigarette would pass the spot on her neck; it would go out of his sight and then it would pass again, going back down to the table; in a second a straight line of smoke would blow in his face. After it had blown at him three or four times, he looked at her. She had a bold game-hen expression and small eyes pointed directly on him.

"If you've been redeemed," he said, "I wouldn't want to be." Then he turned his head to the window. He saw his pale reflection with the dark empty space outside coming through it. A boxcar roared past, chopping the empty space in two, and one of the women laughed.

"Do you think I believe in Jesus?" he said, leaning toward her and speaking almost as if he were breathless. "Well I wouldn't even if He existed. Even if He was on this train."

"Who said you had to?" she asked in a poisonous Eastern voice.

He drew back.

The waiter brought his dinner. He began eating slowly at first, then faster as the women concentrated on watching the muscles that stood out on his jaw when he chewed. He was eating something spotted with eggs and livers. He finished that and drank his coffee and then pulled his money out. The steward saw him but he wouldn't come total the bill. Every time he passed the table, he would wink at the women and stare at Haze. Mrs. Hitchcock and the lady had already finished and gone. Finally the man came and added up the bill. Haze shoved the money at him and then pushed past him out of the car.

For a while he stood between two train cars where there was fresh air of a sort and made a cigarette. Then the porter passed between the two cars. "Hey you Parrum," he called.

The porter didn't stop.

Haze followed him into the car. All the berths were made up. The man in the station in Melsy had sold him a berth because he said he would have to sit up all night in the coaches; he had sold him an upper one. Haze went to it and pulled his sack down and went into the men's room and got ready for the night. He was too full and he wanted to hurry and get in the berth and lie down. He thought he would lie there and look out the window and watch how the country went by a train at night. A sign said to get the porter to let you into the uppers. He stuck his sack up into his berth and then went to look for the porter. He didn't find him at one end of the car and he started back to the other. Going around the corner he ran into something heavy and pink; it gasped and muttered, "Clumsy!" It was Mrs. Hitchcock in a pink wrapper, with her hair in knots around her head. She looked at him with her eyes squinted nearly shut. The knobs framed her face like dark toadstools. She tried to get past him and he tried to let her but they were both moving the same way each time. Her face became purplish except for little white marks over it that didn't heat up. She drew herself stiff and stopped and said, "What is the matter with you?" He slipped past her and dashed down the aisle and ran into the porter so that the porter fell down.

"You got to let me into the berth, Parrum," he said.

The porter picked himself up and went lurching down the aisle and after a minute he came lurching back again, stone-faced, with the ladder. Haze stood watching him while he put the ladder up; then he started up it. Halfway up, he turned and said, "I remember you. Your father was a nigger named Cash Parrum. You can't go back there neither, nor anybody else, not if they wanted to."

"I'm from Chicago," the porter said in an irritated voice. "My name is not Parrum."

"Cash is dead," Haze said. "He got the cholera from a pig."

The porter's mouth jerked down and he said, "My father was a railroad man."

Haze laughed. The porter jerked the ladder off suddenly with a wrench of his arm that sent the boy clutching at the blanket into the berth. He lay on his stomach for a few minutes and didn't move. After a while he turned and found the light and looked around him. There was no window. He was closed up in the thing except for a little space over the curtain. The top of the berth was low and curved over. He lay down and noticed that the curved top looked as if it were not quite closed; it looked as if it were closing. He lay there for a while, not moving. There was something in his throat like a sponge with an egg taste; he didn't want to turn over for fear it would move. He wanted the light off. He reached up without turning and felt for the button and snapped it and the darkness sank down on him and then faded a little with light from the aisle that came in through the foot of space not closed. He wanted it all dark, he didn't want it diluted. He heard the porter's footsteps coming down the aisle, soft into the rug, coming steadily down, brushing against the green curtains and fading up the other way out of hearing. Then after a while when he was almost asleep, he thought he heard them again coming back. His curtains stirred and the footsteps faded.

In his half-sleep he thought where he was lying was like a coffin. The first coffin he had seen with someone in it was his grandfather's. They had left it propped open with a stick of kindling the night it had sat in the house with the old man in it, and Haze had watched from a distance, thinking: he ain't going to let them shut it on him; when the time comes, his elbow is going to shoot into the crack. His grandfather had been a circuit preacher, a waspish old man who had ridden over three counties with Jesus hidden in his head like a stinger. When it was time to bury him, they shut the top of his box down and he didn't make a move.

Haze had had two younger brothers; one died in infancy and was put in a small box. The other fell in front of a mowing machine when he was seven. His box was about half the size of an ordinary one, and when they shut it, Haze ran and opened it up again. They said it was because he was heartbroken to part with his brother, but it was not; it was because he had thought, what if he had been in it and they had shut it on him.

He was asleep now and he dreamed he was at his father's burying again. He saw him humped over on his hands and knees in his coffin, being carried that way to the graveyard. "If I keep my can in the air," he heard the old man say, "nobody can shut nothing on me," but when they got his box to the hole, they let it drop down with a thud and his father flattened out like anybody else. The train jolted and stirred him half awake again and he thought, there must have been twenty-five people in Eastrod then, three

Motes. Now there were no more Motes, no more Ashfields, no more Blasengames, Feys, Jacksons . . . or Parrums—even niggers wouldn't have it. Turning in the road, he saw in the dark the store boarded and the barn leaning and the smaller house half carted away, the porch gone and no floor in the hall.

It had not been that way when he was eighteen years old and had left it. Then there had been ten people there and he had not noticed that it had got smaller from his father's time. He had left it when he was eighteen years old because the army had called him. He had thought at first he would shoot his foot and not go. He was going to be a preacher like his grandfather and a preacher can always do without a foot. A preacher's power is in his neck and tongue and arm. His grandfather had traveled three counties in a Ford automobile. Every fourth Saturday he had driven into Eastrod as if he were just in time to save them all from Hell, and he was shouting before he had the car door open. People gathered around his Ford because he seemed to dare them to. He would climb up on the nose of it and preach from there and sometimes he would climb onto the top of it and shout down at them. They were like stones! he would shout. But Jesus had died to redeem them! Jesus was so soul-hungry that He had died, one death for all, but He would have died every soul's death for one! Did they understand that? Did they understand that for each stone soul, He would have died ten million deaths, had His arms and legs stretched on the cross and nailed ten million times for one of them? (The old man would point to his grandson, Haze. He had a particular disrespect for him because his own face was repeated almost exactly in the child's and seemed to mock him.) Did they know that even for that boy there, for that mean sinful unthinking boy standing there with his dirty hands clenching and unclenching at his sides, Jesus would die ten million deaths before He would let him lose his soul? He would chase him over the waters of sin! Did they doubt Jesus could walk on the waters of sin? That boy had been redeemed and Jesus wasn't going to leave him ever. Jesus would never let him forget he was redeemed. What did the sinner think there was to be gained? Jesus would have him in the end!

The boy didn't need to hear it. There was already a deep black wordless conviction in him that the way to avoid Jesus was to avoid sin. He knew by the time he was twelve years old that he was going to be a preacher. Later he saw Jesus move from tree to tree in the back of his mind, a wild ragged figure motioning him to turn around and come off into the dark where he was not sure of his footing, where he might be walking on the water and not know it and then suddenly know it and drown. Where he wanted to stay was in Eastrod with his two eyes open, and his hands always handling the familiar thing, his feet on the known track, and his tongue not too loose. When he was eighteen and the army called him, he saw the war as a trick to lead him into temptation, and he would have shot his foot except that he trusted himself to get back in a few months, uncorrupted. He had a strong confidence in his power to resist evil; it was something he had inherited, like his face, from his grandfather. He thought that if the government wasn't through with him in four months, he would leave anyway. He had thought, then when he was eighteen years old, that he would give them exactly four months of his time. He was gone four years; he didn't get back, even for a visit.

The only things from Eastrod he took into the army with him were a black Bible and a pair of silver-rimmed spectacles that had belonged to his mother. He had gone to a country school where he had learned to read and write but that it was wiser not to; the Bible was the only book he read. He didn't read it often but when he did he wore his mother's glasses. They tired his eyes so that after a short time he was always obliged to stop. He meant to tell anyone in the army who invited him to sin that he was from Eastrod, Tennessee, and that he meant to get back there and stay back there, that he was going to be a preacher of the gospel and that he wasn't going to have his soul damned by the government or by any foreign place it sent him to.

After a few weeks in the camp, when he had some friends—they were not actually friends but he had to live with them—he was offered the chance he had been waiting for; the invitation. He took his mother's glasses out of his pocket and put them on. Then he told them he wouldn't go with them for a million dollars and a feather bed to lie on; he said he was from Eastrod, Tennessee, and that he was not going to have his soul damned by the government or any foreign place they . . . but his voice cracked and he didn't finish. He only stared at them, trying to steel his face. His friends told him that nobody was interested in his goddam soul unless it was the priest and he managed to answer that no priest taking orders from no pope was going to tamper with his soul. They told him he didn't have any soul and left for their brothel.

He took a long time to believe them because he wanted to believe them. All he wanted was to believe them and get rid of it once and for all, and he saw the opportunity here to get rid of it without corruption, to be converted to nothing instead of to evil. The army sent him halfway around the world and forgot him. He was wounded and they remembered him long enough to take the shrapnel out of his chest—they said they took it out but they never showed it to him and he felt it still in there, rusted, and poisoning him—and then they sent him to another desert and forgot him again. He had all the time he could want to study his soul in and assure himself that it was not there. When he was thoroughly convinced, he saw that this was something that he had always known. The misery he had was a longing for home; it had nothing to do with Jesus.

When the army finally let him go, he was pleased to think that he was still uncorrupted. All he wanted was to get back to Eastrod, Tennessee. The black Bible and his mother's glasses were still in the bottom of his duffel bag. He didn't read any book now but he kept the Bible because it had come from home. He kept the glasses in case his vision should ever become dim.

When the army had released him two days before in a city about three hundred miles north of where he wanted to be, he had gone immediately to the railroad station there and bought a ticket to Melsy, the nearest railroad stop to Eastrod. Then since he had to wait four hours for the train, he went into a dark dry-goods store near the station. It was a thin cardboard-smelling store that got darker as it got deeper. He went deep into it and was sold a blue suit and a dark hat. He had his army suit put in a paper sack and he stuffed it into a trashbox on the corner. Once outside in the light, the new suit turned glare-blue and the lines of the hat seemed to stiffen fiercely.

He was in Melsy at five o'clock in the afternoon and he caught a ride on a cotton-seed truck that took him more than half the distance to Eastrod. He walked the rest of the way and got there at nine o'clock at night, when it had just got dark. The house was as dark as the night and open to it and though he saw that the fence around it had partly fallen and that weeds were growing through the porch floor, he didn't realize all at once that it was only a shell, that there was nothing here but the skeleton of a house. He twisted an envelope and struck a match to it and went through all the empty rooms, upstairs and down. When the envelope burnt out, he lit another one and went through them all again. That night he slept on the floor in the kitchen, and a board fell on his head out of the roof and cut his face.

There was nothing left in the house but the chifforobe in the kitchen. His mother had always slept in the kitchen and had her walnut chifforobe in there. She had given thirty dollars for it and hadn't bought herself anything else big again. Whoever had got everything else, had left that. He opened all the drawers. There were two lengths of wrapping cord in the top one and nothing in the others. He was surprised nobody had come and stolen a chifforobe like that. He took the wrapping cord and tied it around the legs and through the floor boards and left a piece of paper in each of the drawers: THIS SHIFFER-ROBE BELONGS TO HAZEL MOTES. DO NOT STEAL IT OR YOU WILL BE HUNTED DOWN AND KILLED.

He thought about the chifforobe in his half-sleep and decided his mother would rest easier in her grave, knowing it was guarded. If she came looking any time at night, she would see. He wondered if she walked at night and came there ever. She would come with that look on her face, unrested and looking; the same look he had seen through the crack of her coffin. He had seen her face through the crack when they were shutting the top on her. He was sixteen then. He had seen the shadow that came down over her face and pulled her mouth down as if she wasn't any more satisfied dead than alive, as if she were going to spring up and shove the lid back and fly out and satisfy herself: but they shut it. She might have been going to fly out of there, she might have been going to spring. He saw her in his sleep, terrible, like a huge bat, dart from the closing, fly out of there, but it was falling dark on top of her, closing down all the time. From inside he saw it closing, coming closer closer down and cutting off the light and the room. He opened his eyes and saw it closing and he sprang up between the crack and wedged his head and shoulders through it and hung there, dizzy, with the dim light of the train slowly showing the rug below. He hung there over the top of the berth curtain and saw the porter at the other end of the car, a white shape in the darkness, standing there watching him and not moving.

"I'm sick!" he called. "I can't be closed up in this thing. Get me out!"

The porter stood watching him and didn't move.

"Jesus," Haze said, "Jesus."

The porter didn't move. "Jesus been a long time gone," he said in a sour triumphant voice.

CHAPTER 2

He didn't get to the city until six the next evening. That morning he had got off the train at a junction stop to get some air and while he had been looking the other way, the train had slid off. He had run after it but his hat had blown away and he had had to run in the other direction to save the hat. Fortunately, he had carried his duffel bag out with him lest someone should steal something out of it. He had to wait six hours at the junction stop until the right train came.

When he got to Taulkinham, as soon as he stepped off the train, he began to see signs and lights. PEANUTS, WESTERN UNION, AJAX, TAXI, HOTEL, CANDY. Most of them were electric and moved up and down or blinked frantically. He walked very slowly, carrying his duffel bag by the neck. His head turned to one side and then the other, first toward one sign and then another. He walked the length of the station and then he walked back as if he might be going to get on the train again. His face was stern and determined under the heavy hat. No one observing him would have known that he had no place to go. He walked up and down the crowded waiting room two or three times, but he did not want to sit on the benches there. He wanted a private place to go to.

Finally he pushed open a door at one end of the station where a plain black and white sign said, MEN'S TOILET. WHITE. He went into a narrow room lined on one side with washbasins and on the other with a row of wooden stalls. The walls of this room had once been a bright cheerful yellow but now they were more nearly green and were decorated with handwriting and with various detailed drawings of the parts of the body of both men and women. Some of the stalls had doors on them and on one of the doors, written with what must have been a crayon, was the large word, WELCOME, followed by three exclamation points and something that looked like a snake. Haze entered this one.

He had been sitting in the narrow box for some time, studying the inscriptions on the sides and door, before he noticed one that was to the left over the toilet paper. It was written in a drunken-looking hand. It said,

> Mrs. Leora Watts!
> 60 Buckley Road
> The friendliest bed in town!
> Brother.

After a while he took a pencil out of his pocket and wrote down the address on the back of an envelope.

Outside he got in a yellow taxi and told the driver where he wanted to go. The driver was a small man with a big leather cap on his head and the tip of a cigar coming out from the center of his mouth. They had driven a few blocks before Haze noticed him squinting at him through the rear-view mirror. "You ain't no friend of hers, are you?" the driver asked.

"I never saw her before," Haze said.

"Where'd you hear about her? She don't usually have no preachers for company." He did not disturb the position of the cigar when he spoke; he was able to speak on either side of it.

"I ain't any preacher," Haze said, frowning. "I only seen her name in the toilet."

"You look like a preacher," the driver said. "That hat looks like a preacher's hat."

"It ain't," Haze said, and leaned forward and gripped the back of the front seat. "It's just a hat."

They stopped in front of a small one-story house between a filling station and a vacant lot. Haze got out and paid his fare through the window.

"It ain't only the hat," the driver said. "It's a look in your face somewheres."

"Listen," Haze said, tilting the hat over one eye, "I'm not a preacher."

"I understand," the driver said. "It ain't anybody perfect on this green earth of God's, preachers nor nobody else. And you can tell people better how terrible sin is if you know from your own personal experience."

Haze put his head in at the window, knocking the hat accidentally straight again. He seemed to have knocked his face straight too for it became completely expressionless. "Listen," he said, "get this: I don't believe in anything."

The driver took the stump of cigar out of his mouth. "Not in nothing at all?" he asked, leaving his mouth open after the question.

"I don't have to say it but once to nobody," Haze said.

The driver closed his mouth and after a second he returned the piece of cigar to it. "That's the trouble with you preachers," he said. "You've all got too good to believe in anything," and he drove off with a look of disgust and righteousness.

Haze turned and looked at the house he was going into. It was little more than a shack but there was a warm glow in one front window. He went up on the front porch and put his eye to a convenient crack in the shade, and found himself looking directly at a large white knee. After some time he moved away from the crack and tried the front door. It was not locked and he went into a small dark hall with a door on either side of it. The door to the left was cracked and let out a narrow shaft of light. He moved into the light and looked through the crack.

Mrs. Watts was sitting alone in a white iron bed, cutting her toenails with a large pair of scissors. She was a big woman with very yellow hair and white skin that glistened with a greasy preparation. She had on a pink nightgown that would better have fit a smaller figure.

Haze made a noise with the doorknob and she looked up and observed him standing behind the crack. She had a bold steady penetrating stare. After a minute, she turned it away from him and began cutting her toenails again.

He went in and stood looking around him. There was nothing much in the room but the bed and a bureau and a rocking chair full of dirty clothes. He went to the bureau and fingered a nail file and then an empty jelly glass while he looked into the yellowish mirror and watched Mrs. Watts, slightly distorted, grinning at him. His senses were stirred to the limit. He turned quickly and went to her bed and sat down on the far corner of it. He drew a long draught of air through one side of his nose and began to run his hand carefully along the sheet.

The pink tip of Mrs. Watts's tongue appeared and moistened her lower lip. She seemed just as glad to see him as if he had been an old friend but she didn't say anything.

He picked up her foot, which was heavy but not cold, and moved it about an inch to one side, and kept his hand on it.

Mrs. Watts's mouth split in a wide full grin that showed her teeth. They were small and pointed and speckled with green and there was a wide space between each one. She reached out and gripped Haze's arm just above the elbow. "You huntin' something?" she drawled.

If she had not had him so firmly by the arm, he might have leaped out the window. Involuntarily his lips formed the words, "Yes, mam," but no sound came through them.

"Something on your mind?" Mrs. Watts asked, pulling his rigid figure a little closer.

"Listen," he said, keeping his voice tightly under control, "I come for the usual business."

Mrs. Watts's mouth became more round, as if she were perplexed at this waste of words. "Make yourself at home," she said simply.

They stared at each other for almost a minute and neither moved. Then he said in a voice that was higher than his usual voice, "What I mean to have you know is: I'm no goddam preacher."

Mrs. Watts eyed him steadily with only a slight smirk. Then she put her other hand under his face and tickled it in a motherly way. "That's okay, son," she said. "Momma don't mind if you ain't a preacher."

CHAPTER 3

His second night in Taulkinham, Hazel Motes walked along down town close to the store fronts but not looking in them. The black sky was underpinned with long silver streaks that looked like scaffolding and depth on depth behind it were thousands of stars that all seemed to be moving very slowly as if they were about some vast construction work that involved the whole order of the universe and would take all time to complete. No one was paying any attention to the sky. The stores in Taulkinham stayed open on Thursday nights so that people could have an extra opportunity to see what was for sale. Haze's shadow was now behind him and now before him and now and then broken up by other people's shadows, but when it was by itself, stretching behind him, it was a thin nervous shadow walking backwards. His neck was thrust forward as if he were trying to smell something that was always being drawn away. The glary light from the store windows made his blue suit look purple.

33

After a while he stopped where a lean-faced man had a card table set up in front of a department store and was demonstrating a potato peeler. The man had on a small canvas hat and a shirt patterned with bunches of upside-down pheasants and quail and bronze turkeys. He was pitching his voice under the street noises so that it reached every ear distinctly as if in a private conversation. A few people gathered around. There were two buckets on the card table, one empty and the other full of potatoes. Between the two buckets there was a pyramid of green cardboard boxes and, on top of the stack, one peeler was open for demonstration. The man stood in front of this altar, pointing over it at various people. "How about you?" he said, pointing at a damp-haired pimpled boy. "You ain't gonna let one of these go by?" He stuck a brown potato in one side of the open machine. The machine was a square tin box with a red handle, and as he turned the handle, the potato went into the box and then in a second, backed out the other side, white. "You ain't gonna let one of these go by!" he said.

The boy guffawed and looked at the other people gathered around. He had yellow hair and a fox-shaped face.

"What's yer name?" the peeler man asked.

"Name Enoch Emery," the boy said and snuffled.

"Boy with a pretty name like that ought to have one of these," the man said, rolling his eyes, trying to warm up the others. Nobody laughed but the boy. Then a man standing across from Hazel Motes laughed, not a pleasant laugh but one that had a sharp edge. He was a tall cadaverous man with a black suit and a black hat on. He had on dark glasses and his cheeks were streaked with lines that looked as if they had been painted on and had faded. They gave him the expression of a grinning mandrill. As soon as he laughed, he began to move forward in a deliberate way, jiggling a tin cup in one hand and tapping a white cane in front of him with the other. Just behind him there came a child, handing out leaflets. She had on a black dress and a black knitted cap pulled down low on her forehead; there was a fringe of brown hair sticking out from it on either side; she had a long face and a short sharp nose. The man selling peelers was irritated when he saw the people looking at this pair instead of him. "How about you, you there," he said, pointing at Haze. "You'll never be able to get a bargain like this in any store."

Haze was looking at the blind man and the child. "Hey!" Enoch Emery said, reaching across a woman and punching his arm. "He's talking to you! He's talking to you!" Enoch had to punch him again before he looked at the peeler man.

"Whyn't you take one of these home to yer wife?" the peeler man was saying.

"Don't have one," Haze muttered, looking back at the blind man again.

"Well, you got a dear old mother, ain't you?"

"No."

"Well pshaw," the man said, with his hand cupped to the people, "he needs one theseyer just to keep him company."

Enoch Emery thought that was so funny that he doubled over and slapped his knee, but Hazel Motes didn't look as if he had heard it yet. "I'm going to give away a half a dozen peeled potatoes to the first person purchasing one theseyer machines," the man said. "Who's gonna step up first? Only a dollar and a half for a machine'd cost you three dollars in any store!" Enoch Emery began fumbling in his pockets. "You'll thank the day you ever stopped here," the man said, "you'll never forget it. Ever' one of you people purchasing one theseyer machines'll never forget it!"

The blind man was moving forward slowly, saying in a kind of garbled mutter, "Help a blind preacher. If you won't repent, give up a nickel. I can use it as good as you. Help a blind unemployed preacher. Wouldn't you rather have me beg than preach? Come on and give a nickel if you won't repent."

There were not many people gathered around but the ones who were began to move off. When the machine-seller saw this, he leaned, glaring over the card table. "Hey you!" he yelled at the blind man. "What you think you doing? Who you think you are, running people off from here?" The blind man didn't pay any attention to him. He kept on rattling the cup and the child kept on handing out the pamphlets. He passed Enoch Emery and came on toward Haze, hitting the white cane out at an angle from his leg. Haze leaned forward and saw that the lines on his face were not painted on; they were scars.

"What the hell you think you doing?" the man selling peelers yelled. "I got these people together, how you think you can horn in?"

The child held one of the pamphlets out to Haze and he grabbed it. The words on the outside of it said, "Jesus Calls You."

"I'd like to know who the hell you think you are!" the man with the peelers was yelling. The child went back to where he was and handed him a tract. He looked at it for an instant with his lip curled and then he charged around the card table, upsetting the bucket of potatoes. "These damn Jesus fanatics," he yelled, glaring around, trying to find the blind man. New people gathered, hoping to see a disturbance. "These goddam Communist foreigners!" the peeler man screamed. "I got this crowd together!" He stopped, realizing there was a crowd.

"Listen folks," he said, "one at a time, there's plenty to go around, just don't push, a half a dozen peeled potatoes to the first person stepping up to buy." He got back behind the card table quietly and started holding up the peeler boxes. "Step on up, plenty to go around," he said, "no need to crowd."

Haze didn't open his tract. He looked at the outside of it and then he tore it across. He put the two pieces together and tore them across again. He kept re-stacking the pieces and tearing them again until he had a little handful of confetti. He turned his hand over and let the shredded leaflet sprinkle to the ground. Then he looked up and saw the blind man's child not three feet away, watching him. Her mouth was open and her eyes glittered on him like two chips of green bottle glass. She had a white gunny sack hung over her shoulder. Haze scowled and began rubbing his sticky hands on his pants.

"I seen you," she said. Then she moved quickly over to where the blind man was standing now, beside the card table, and turned her head and looked at Haze from there. Most of the people had moved off.

The peeler man leaned over the card table and said, "Hey!" to the blind man. "I reckon that showed you. Trying to horn in."

"Lookerhere," Enoch Emery said, "I ain't got but a dollar sixteen cent but I . . ."

"Yah," the man said, "I reckon that'll show you you can't muscle in on me. Sold eight peelers, sold . . ."

"Give me one of them," the blind man's child said, pointing to the peelers.

"Hanh," he said.

She was untying a handkerchief. She untied two fifty-cent pieces out of the knotted corner of it. "Give me one of them," she said, holding out the money.

The man eyed it with his mouth hiked to one side. "A buck fifty, sister," he said.

She pulled her hand in quickly and all at once glared at Hazel Motes as if he had made a noise at her. The blind man was moving on. She stood a second glaring at Haze, and then she turned and followed the blind man. Haze started.

"Listen," Enoch Emery said, "I ain't got but a dollar sixteen cent and I want me one of them . . ."

"You can keep it," the man said, taking the bucket off the card table. "This ain't no cut-rate joint."

Haze could see the blind man moving down the street some distance away. He stood staring after him, jerking his hands in and out of his pockets as if he were trying to move forward and backward at the same time. Then suddenly he thrust two dollars at the man selling peelers and snatched a box off the card table and started running down the street. In a second Enoch Emery was panting at his elbow. "My, I reckon you got a heap of money," Enoch Emery said.

Haze saw the child catch up with the blind man and take him by the elbow. They were about a block ahead of him. He slowed down some and saw Enoch Emery there. Enoch had on a yellowish white suit and a pinkish white shirt and his tie was the color of green peas. He was smiling. He looked like a friendly hound dog with light mange. "How long you been here?" he inquired.

"Two days," Haze muttered.

"I been here two months," Enoch said. "I work for the city. Where you work?"

"Not working," Haze said.

"That's too bad," Enoch said. "I work for the city." He skipped a step to get in line with Haze, then he said, "I'm eighteen year old and I ain't been here but two months and I already work for the city."

"That's fine," Haze said. He pulled his hat down farther on the side Enoch Emery was on and walked very fast. The blind man up ahead began to make mock bows to the right and left.

"I didn't ketch your name good," Enoch said.

Haze said his name.

"You look like you might be follerin' them hicks," Enoch remarked. "You go in for a lot of Jesus business?"

"No," Haze said.

"No, me neither, not much," Enoch agreed. "I went to thisyer Rodemill Boys' Bible Academy for four weeks. Thisyer woman that traded me from my daddy she sent me. She was a Welfare woman. Jesus, four weeks and I thought I was going to be sanctified crazy."

Haze walked to the end of the block and Enoch stayed at his elbow, panting and talking. When Haze started across the street, Enoch yelled, "Don't you see theter light! That means you got to wait!" A cop blew a whistle and a car blasted its horn and stopped short. Haze went on across, keeping his eyes on the blind man in the middle of the block. The policeman kept on blowing his whistle. He crossed the street to where Haze was and stopped him. He had a thin face and oval-shaped yellow eyes.

"You know what that little thing hanging up there is for?" he asked, pointing to the traffic light over the inter-section.

"I didn't see it," Haze said.

The policeman looked at him without saying anything. A few people stopped. He rolled his eyes at them. "Maybe you thought the red ones was for white folks and the green ones for niggers," he said.

"Yeah I thought that," Haze said. "Take your hand off me."

The policeman took his hand off and put it on his hip. He backed one step away and said, "You tell all your friends about these lights. Red is to stop, green is to go—men and women, white folks and niggers, all go on the same light. You tell all your friends so when they come to town, they'll know." The people laughed.

"I'll look after him," Enoch Emery said, pushing in by the policeman. "He ain't been here but only two days. I'll look after him."

"How long you been here?" the cop asked.

"I was born and raised here," Enoch said. "This is my

ol' home town. I'll take care of him for you. Hey wait!"
he yelled at Haze. "Wait on me!" He pushed out of the
crowd and caught up with him. "I reckon I saved you that
time," he said.

"I'm obliged," Haze said.

"It wasn't nothing," Enoch said. "Whyn't we go in Walgreen's and get us a soda? Ain't no night clubs open this
early."

"I don't like drug stores," Haze said. "Good-by."

"That's all right," Enoch said. "I reckon I'll go along
and keep you company for a while." He looked up ahead at
the blind man and the child and said, "I sho wouldn't
want to get messed up with no hicks this time of night,
particularly the Jesus kind. I done had enough of them
myself. Thisyer Welfare woman that traded me from my
daddy didn't do nothing but pray. Me and daddy we moved
around with a sawmill where we worked and it set up outside Boonville one summer and here come thisyer woman."
He caught hold of Haze's coat. "Only objection I got to
Taulkinham is there's too many people on the streets,"
he said confidentially. "Look like all they want to do is
knock you down—well here she come and I reckon she took
a fancy to me. I was twelve year old and I could sing some
hymns good I learnt off a nigger. So here she comes taking
a fancy to me and traded me off my daddy and took me to
Boonville to live with her. She had a brick house but it
was Jesus all day long." A little man lost in a pair of faded

42

overalls jostled him. "Whyn't you look wher you going?" Enoch growled.

The little man stopped and raised his arm in a vicious gesture and a nasty-dog look came on his face. "Who you tellin' what?" he snarled.

"You see," Enoch said, jumping to catch up with Haze, "all they want to do is knock you down. I ain't never been to such a unfriendly place before. Even with that woman. I stayed with her for two months in that house of hers," he went on, "and then come fall she sent me to the Rodemill Boys' Bible Academy and I thought that sho was going to be some relief. This woman was hard to get along with— she wasn't old, I reckon she was forty year old—but she sho was ugly. She had theseyer brown glasses and her hair was so thin it looked like ham gravy trickling over her skull. I thought it was going to be some certain relief to get to theter Academy. I had run away oncet on her and she got me back and come to find out she had papers on me and she could send me to the penitentiary if I didn't stay with her so I sho was glad to get to theter Academy. You ever been to a academy?"

Haze didn't seem to hear the question.

"Well, it won't no relief," Enoch said. "Good Jesus, it won't no relief. I run away from there after four weeks and durn if she didn't get me back and brought me to that house of hers again. I got out though." He waited a minute. "You want to know how?"

After a second he said, "I scared hell out of that woman, that's how. I studied on it and studied on it. I even prayed. I said, 'Jesus, show me the way to get out of here without killing thisyer woman and getting sent to the penitentiary,' and durn if He didn't. I got up one morning at just daylight and I went in her room without my pants on and pulled the sheet off her and giver a heart attact. Then I went back to my daddy and we ain't seen hide of her since.

"Your jaw just crawls," he observed, watching the side of Haze's face. "You don't never laugh. I wouldn't be surprised if you wasn't a real wealthy man."

Haze turned down a side street. The blind man and the girl were on the corner a block ahead. "Well, I reckon we going to ketch up with them after all," Enoch said. "You know many people here?"

"No," Haze said.

"You ain't gonna know none neither. This is one more hard place to make friends in. I been here two months and I don't know nobody. Look like all they want to do is knock you down. I reckon you got a right heap of money," he said. "I ain't got none. Had, I'd sho know what to do with it." The blind man and his child stopped on the corner and turned up the left side of the street. "We ketchin' up," he said. "I bet we'll be at some meeting singing hymns with her and her daddy if we don't watch out."

Up in the next block there was a large building with columns and a dome. The blind man and the girl were going toward it. There was a car parked in every space around the building and on the other side of the street and up and down the streets near it. "That ain't no picture show," Enoch said. The blind man and the girl turned up the steps to the building. The steps went all the way across the front, and on either side there were stone lions sitting on pedestals. "Ain't no church," Enoch said. Haze stopped at the steps. He looked as if he were trying to settle his face into an expression. He pulled the black hat forward at a sharp angle and started toward the two, who had sat down in the corner by one of the lions. He came up to where the blind man was without saying anything and stood leaning forward in front of him as if he were trying to see through the black glasses. The child stared at him.

The blind man's mouth thinned slightly. "I can smell the sin on your breath," he said.

Haze drew back.

"What'd you follow me for?"

"I never followed you," Haze said.

"She said you were following," the blind man said, jerking his thumb in the direction of the child.

"I ain't followed you," Haze said. He felt the peeler box in his hand and looked at the girl. Her black knitted cap made a straight line across her forehead. She grinned suddenly and then quickly drew her expression back together as if she smelled something bad. "I ain't followed you nowhere," Haze said. "I followed her." He stuck the peeler out at her.

At first she looked as if she were going to grab it, but she didn't. "I don't want that thing," she said. "What you think I want with that thing? Take it. It ain't mine. I don't want it!"

"You take it," the blind man said. "You put it in your sack and shut up before I hit you."

Haze thrust the peeler at her again.

"I won't have it," she muttered.

"You take it like I told you," the blind man said. "He never followed you."

She took it and shoved it in the sack where the tracts were. "It ain't mine," she said. "I got it but it ain't mine."

"I followed her to say I ain't beholden for none of her fast eye like she gave me back there," Haze said, looking at the blind man.

"What you mean?" she shouted. "I never looked at you with no fast eye. I only watched you tearing up that tract. He tore it up in little pieces," she said, pushing the blind man's shoulder. "He tore it up and sprinkled it all over the ground like salt and wiped his hands on his pants."

"He followed me," the blind man said. "Nobody would follow you. I can hear the urge for Jesus in his voice."

"Jesus," Haze muttered. "My Jesus." He sat down by the girl's leg and set his hand on the step next to her foot. She had on sneakers and black cotton stockings.

"Listen at him cursing," she said in a low tone. "He never followed you, Papa."

The blind man gave his edgy laugh. "Listen boy," he said, "you can't run away from Jesus. Jesus is a fact."

"I know a whole heap about Jesus," Enoch said. "I attended thisyer Rodemill Boys' Bible Academy that a woman sent me to. If it's anything you want to know about Jesus, just ast me." He had got up on the lion's back and he was sitting there sideways, cross-legged.

"I come a long way," Haze said, "since I would believe anything. I come halfway around the world."

"Me too," Enoch Emery said.

"You ain't come so far that you could keep from following me," the blind man said. He reached out suddenly and his hands covered Haze's face. For a second Haze didn't move or make any sound. Then he knocked the hands off.

"Quit it," he said in a faint voice. "You don't know anything about me."

"My daddy looks just like Jesus," Enoch remarked from the lion's back. "His hair hangs to his shoulders. Only difference is he's got a scar acrost his chin. I ain't never seen who my mother is."

"Some preacher has left his mark on you," the blind man said with a kind of snicker. "Did you follow for me to take it off or give you another one?"

"Listen here, there's nothing for your pain but Jesus,"

the child said suddenly. She tapped Haze on the shoulder. He sat there with his black hat tilted forward over his face. "Listen," she said in a louder voice, "this here man and woman killed this little baby. It was her own child but it was ugly and she never give it any love. This child had Jesus and this woman didn't have nothing but good looks and a man she was living in sin with. She sent the child away and it come back and she sent it away again and it come back again and ever' time she sent it away, it come back to where her and this man was living in sin. They strangled it with a silk stocking and hung it up in the chimney. It didn't give her any peace after that, though. Everything she looked at was that child. Jesus made it beautiful to haunt her. She couldn't lie with that man without she saw it, staring through the chimney at her, shining through the brick in the middle of the night."

"My Jesus," Haze muttered.

"She didn't have nothing but good looks," she said in the loud fast voice. "That ain't enough. No sirree."

"I hear them scraping their feet inside there," the blind man said. "Get out the tracts, they're fixing to come out."

"It ain't enough," she repeated.

"What we gonna do?" Enoch asked. "What's inside theter building?"

"A program letting out," the blind man said. "My congregation."

The child took the tracts out of the gunny sack and gave

him two bunches of them, tied with a string. "You and the other boy go over on that side and give out," he said to her. "Me and the one that followed me'll stay over here."

"He don't have no business touching them," she said. "He don't want to do anything but shred them up."

"Go like I told you," the blind man said.

She stood there a second, scowling. Then she said, "You come on if you're coming," to Enoch Emery and Enoch jumped off the lion and followed her over to the other side.

Haze ducked down a step but the blind man's hand shot out and clamped him around the arm. He said in a fast whisper, "Repent! Go to the head of the stairs and renounce your sins and distribute these tracts to the people!" and he thrust a stack of pamphlets into Haze's hand.

Haze jerked his arm away but he only pulled the blind man nearer. "Listen," he said, "I'm as clean as you are."

"Fornication and blasphemy and what else?" the blind man said.

"They ain't nothing but words," Haze said. "If I was in sin I was in it before I ever committed any. There's no change come in me." He was trying to pry the fingers off from around his arm but the blind man kept wrapping them tighter. "I don't believe in sin," Haze said, "take your hand off me."

"Jesus loves you," the blind man said in a flat mocking voice, "Jesus loves you, Jesus loves you . . ."

"Nothing matters but that Jesus don't exist," Haze said, pulling his arm free.

"Go to the head of the stairs and distribute these tracts and . . ."

"I'll take them up there and throw them over into the bushes!" Haze shouted. "You be watching and see can you see."

"I can see more than you!" the blind man yelled, laughing. "You got eyes and see not, ears and hear not, but you'll have to see some time."

"You be watching if you can see!" Haze said, and started running up the steps. A crowd of people were already coming out the auditorium doors and some were halfway down the steps. He pushed through them with his elbows out like sharp wings and when he got to the top, a new surge of them pushed him back almost to where he had started up. He fought through them again until somebody shouted, "Make room for this idiot!" and people got out of his way. He rushed to the top and pushed his way over to the side and stood there, glaring and panting.

"I never followed him," he said aloud. "I wouldn't follow a blind fool like that. My Jesus." He stood against the building, holding the stack of leaflets by the string. A fat man stopped near him to light a cigar and Haze pushed his shoulder. "Look down yonder," he said. "See that blind man down there? He's giving out tracts and begging. Jesus. You ought to see him and he's got this here ugly child dressed up in woman's clothes, giving them out too. My Jesus."

"There's always fanatics," the fat man said, moving on.

"My Jesus," Haze said. He leaned forward near an old woman with blue hair and a collar of red wooden beads. "You better get on the other side, lady," he said. "There's a fool down there giving out tracts." The crowd behind the old woman pushed her on, but she looked at him for an instant with two bright flea eyes. He started toward her through the people but she was already too far away and he pushed back to where he had been standing against the wall. "Sweet Jesus Christ Crucified," he said, "I want to tell you people something. Maybe you think you're not clean because you don't believe. Well you are clean, let me tell you that. Every one of you people are clean and let me tell you why if you think it's because of Jesus Christ Crucified you're wrong. I don't say he wasn't crucified but I say it wasn't for you. Listenhere, I'm a preacher myself and I preach the truth." The crowd was moving fast. It was like a large spread raveling and the separate threads disappeared down the dark streets. "Don't I know what exists and what don't?" he cried. "Don't I have eyes in my head? Am I a blind man? Listenhere," he called, "I'm going to preach a new church—the church of truth without Jesus Christ Crucified. It won't cost you nothing to join my church. It's not started yet but it's going to be." The few people who were left glanced at him once or twice. There were tracts scattered below over the sidewalk and out on the street. The blind man was sitting on the bottom step. Enoch Emery was on the other side, standing on the lion's head, trying to balance himself, and the child was standing near him, watching Haze. "I don't need Jesus," Haze said. "What do I need with Jesus? I got Leora Watts."

He went down the stairs quietly to where the blind man was and stopped. He stood there a second and the blind man laughed. Haze moved away, and started across the street. He was on the other side before the voice pierced after him. He turned and saw the blind man standing in the middle of the street, shouting, "Hawks, Hawks, my name is Asa Hawks when you try to follow me again!" A car had to swerve to the side to keep from hitting him. "Repent!" he shouted and laughed and ran forward a little way, pretending he was going to come after Haze and grab him.

Haze drew his head down nearer his hunched shoulders and went on quickly. He didn't look back until he heard other footsteps coming behind him.

"Now that we got shut of them," Enoch Emery panted, "whyn't we go somewher and have us some fun?"

"Listen," Haze said roughly, "I got business of my own. I seen all of you I want." He began walking very fast.

Enoch kept skipping steps to keep up. "I been here two months," he said, "and I don't know nobody. People ain't friendly here. I got me a room and there ain't never nobody in it but me. My daddy said I had to come. I wouldn't never have come but he made me. I think I seen you sommers before. You ain't from Stockwell, are you?"

"No."

"Melsy?"

"No."

"Sawmill set up there oncet," Enoch said. "Look like you had a kind of familer face."

They walked on without saying anything until they got on the main street again. It was almost deserted. "Good-by," Haze said.

"I'm going thisaway too," Enoch said in a sullen voice. On the left there was a movie house where the electric bill was being changed. "We hadn't got tied up with them hicks we could have gone to a show," he muttered: He strode along at Haze's elbow, talking in a half mumble, half whine. Once he caught at his sleeve to slow him down and Haze jerked it away. "My daddy made me come," he said in a cracked voice. Haze looked at him and saw he was crying, his face seamed and wet and a purple-pink color. "I ain't but eighteen year old," he cried, "an' he made me come and I don't know nobody, nobody here'll have nothing to do with nobody else. They ain't friendly. He done gone off with a woman and made me come but she ain't going to stay for long, he'll beat hell out of her before she gets herself stuck to a chair. You the first familer face I seen in two months. I seen you sommers before. I know I seen you sommers before."

Haze looked straight ahead with his face set and Enoch kept up the half mumble, half blubber. They passed a church and a hotel and an antique shop and turned up Mrs. Watts's street.

"If you want you a woman you don't have to be follering nothing looked like that kid you give a peeler to," Enoch said. "I heard about where there's a house where we could have us some fun. I could pay you back next week."

"Look," Haze said, "I'm going where I'm going—two doors from here. I got a woman. I got a woman, see? And that's where I'm going—to visit her. I don't need to go with you."

"I could pay you back next week," Enoch said. "I work at the city zoo. I guard a gate and I get paid ever' week."

"Get away from me," Haze said.

"People ain't friendly here. You ain't from here but you ain't friendly neither."

Haze didn't answer him. He went on with his neck drawn close to his shoulder blades as if he were cold.

"You don't know nobody neither," Enoch said. "You ain't got no woman nor nothing to do. I knew when I first seen you you didn't have nobody nor nothing but Jesus. I seen you and I knew it."

"This is where I'm going in at," Haze said, and he turned up the walk without looking back at Enoch.

Enoch stopped. "Yeah," he cried, "oh yeah," and he ran his sleeve under his nose to stop the snivel. "Yeah," he cried, "go on where you goin' but lookerhere." He slapped at his pocket and ran up and caught Haze's sleeve and rattled the peeler box at him. "She give me this. She give it to me and there ain't nothing you can do about it. She told me where they lived and ast me to visit them and bring you—not you bring me, me bring you—and it was you follerin' them." His eyes glinted through his tears and his face stretched in an evil crooked grin. "You act like you think you got wiser blood than anybody else," he said, "but you ain't! I'm the one has it. Not you. *Me.*"

Haze didn't say anything. He stood there for an instant, small in the middle of the steps, and then he raised his arm and hurled the stack of tracts he had been carrying. It hit Enoch in the chest and knocked his mouth open. He stood looking, with his mouth hanging open, at where it had hit his front, and then he turned and tore off down the street; and Haze went into the house.

Since the night before was the first time he had slept with any woman, he had not been very successful with Mrs. Watts. When he finished, he was like something washed ashore on her, and she had made obscene comments about him, which he remembered off and on during the day. He was uneasy in the thought of going to her again. He didn't know what she would say when he opened the door and she saw him there.

When he opened the door and she saw him there, she said, "Ha ha."

The black hat sat on his head squarely. He came in with it on and when it knocked the electric light bulb that hung down from the middle of the ceiling, he took it off. Mrs. Watts was in bed, applying a grease to her face. She rested her chin on her hand and watched him. He began to move around the room, examining this and that. His throat got dryer and his heart began to grip him like a little ape clutching the bars of its cage. He sat down on the edge of her bed, with his hat in his hand.

Mrs. Watts's grin was as curved and sharp as the blade of a sickle. It was plain that she was so well-adjusted that she didn't have to think any more. Her eyes took everything in whole, like quicksand. "That Jesus-seeing hat!" she said. She sat up and pulled her nightgown from under her and took it off. She reached for his hat and put it on her head and sat with her hands on her hips, walling her eyes in a comical way. Haze stared for a minute, then he made three quick noises that were laughs. He jumped for the electric light cord and took off his clothes in the dark.

Once when he was small, his father took him to a carnival that stopped in Melsy. There was one tent that cost more money a little off to one side. A dried-up man with a horn voice was barking it. He didn't say what was inside. He said it was so SINsational that it would cost any man that wanted to see it thirty-five cents, and it was so EXclusive, only fifteen could get in at a time. His father sent him to a tent where two monkeys danced, and then he made for it, moving close to the walls of things like he moved. Haze left the monkeys and followed him, but he didn't have thirty-five cents. He asked the barker what was inside.

"Beat it," the man said. "There ain't no pop and there ain't no monkeys."

"I already seen them," he said.

"That's fine," the man said, "beat it."

"I got fifteen cents," he said. "Whyn't you lemme in and I could see half of it?" It's something about a privy, he was thinking. It's some men in a privy. Then he thought, maybe it's a man and a woman in a privy. She wouldn't want me in there. "I got fifteen cents," he said.

"It's more than half over," the man said, fanning with his straw hat. "You run along."

"That'll be fifteen cents worth then," Haze said.

"Scram," the man said.

"Is it a nigger?" Haze asked. "Are they doing something to a nigger?"

The man leaned off his platform and his dried-up face drew into a glare. "Where'd you get that idear?" he said.

"I don't know," Haze said.

"How old are you?" the man asked.

"Twelve," Haze said. He was ten.

"Gimme that fifteen cents," the man said, "and get in there."

He slid the money on the platform and scrambled to get in before it was over. He went through the flap of the tent and inside there was another tent and he went through that. All he could see were the backs of the men. He climbed up·on a bench and looked over their heads. They were looking down into a lowered place where something white was lying, squirming a little, in a box lined with black cloth. For a second he thought it was a skinned animal and then he saw it was a woman. She was fat and she had a face like an ordinary woman except there was a mole on the corner of her lip, that moved when she grinned, and one on her side.

"Had one of themther built into ever' casket," his father, up toward the front, said, "be a heap ready to go sooner."

Haze recognized the voice without looking. He slid down off the bench and scrambled out of the tent. He crawled out under the side of the outside one because he didn't want to pass the barker. He got in the back of a truck and sat down in the far corner of it. The carnival was making a tin roar outside.

His mother was standing by the washpot in the yard, looking at him, when he got home. She wore black all the time and her dresses were longer than other women's. She was standing there straight, looking at him. He moved behind a tree and got out of her view, but in a few minutes, he could feel her watching him through the tree. He saw the lowered place and the casket again and a thin woman in the casket who was too long for it. Her head stuck up at one end and her knees were raised to make her fit. She had a cross-shaped face and hair pulled close to her head. He stood flat against the tree, waiting. She left the wash-pot and came toward him with a stick. She said, "What you seen?

"What you seen?" she said.

"What you seen," she said, using the same tone of voice all the time. She hit him across the legs with the stick, but he was like part of the tree. "Jesus died to redeem you," she said.

"I never ast him," he muttered.

She didn't hit him again but she stood looking at him, shut-mouthed, and he forgot the guilt of the tent for the nameless unplaced guilt that was in him. In a minute she threw the stick away from her and went back to the wash-pot, still shut-mouthed.

The next day he took his shoes in secret out into the woods. He didn't wear them except for revivals and in the winter. He took them out of the box and filled the bottoms of them with stones and small rocks and then he put them on. He laced them up tight and walked in them through the woods for what he knew to be a mile, until he came to a creek, and then he sat down and took them off and eased his feet in the wet sand. He thought, that ought to satisfy

Him. Nothing happened. If a stone had fallen he would have taken it as a sign. After a while he drew his feet out of the sand and let them dry, and then he put the shoes on again with the rocks still in them and he walked a half-mile back before he took them off.

CHAPTER 4

He got out of Mrs. Watts's bed early in the morning before any light came in the room. When he woke up, her arm was flung across him. He leaned up and lifted it off and eased it down by her side, but he didn't look at her. There was only one thought in his mind: he was going to buy a car. The thought was full grown in his head when he woke up, and he didn't think of anything else. He had never thought before of buying a car; he had never even wanted one before. He had driven one only a little in his life and he didn't have any license. He had only fifty dollars but he thought he could buy a car for that. He got stealthily out the bed, without disturbing Mrs. Watts, and put his clothes on silently. By six-thirty, he was down town, looking for used-car lots.

Used-car lots were scattered among the blocks of old buildings that separated the business section from the railroad yards. He wandered around in a few of them before they were open. He could tell from the outside of the lot if it would have a fifty-dollar car in it. When they began to be open for business, he went through them quickly, paying no attention to anyone who tried to show him the stock. His black hat sat on his head with a careful, placed expression and his face had a fragile look as if it might have been broken and stuck together again, or like a gun no one knows is loaded.

It was a wet glary day. The sky was like a piece of thin polished silver with a dark sour-looking sun in one corner of it. By ten o'clock he had canvassed all the better lots and was nearing the railroad yards. Even here, the lots were full of cars that cost more than fifty dollars. Finally he came to one between two deserted warehouses. A sign over the entrance said: SLADE'S FOR THE LATEST.

There was a gravel road going down the middle of the lot and over to one side near the front, a tin shack with the word, OFFICE, painted on the door. The rest of the lot was full of old cars and broken machinery. A white boy was sitting on a gasoline can in front of the office. He had the look of being there to keep people out. He wore a black raincoat and his face was partly hidden under a leather cap. There was a cigarette hanging out of one corner of his mouth and the ash on it was about an inch long.

Haze started off toward the back of the lot where he saw a particular car. "Hey!" the boy yelled. "You don't just walk in here like that. I'll show you what I got to show," but Haze didn't pay any attention to him. He went on toward the back of the lot where he saw the car. The boy came huffing behind him, cursing. The car he saw was on the last row of cars. It was a high rat-colored machine with large thin wheels and bulging headlights. When he got up to it, he saw that one door was tied on with a rope and that it had an oval window in the back. This was the car he was going to buy.

"Lemme see Slade," he said.

"What you want to see him for?" the boy asked in a testy voice. He had a wide mouth and when he talked he used one side only of it.

"I want to see him about this car," Haze said.

"I'm him," the boy said. His face under the cap was like a thin picked eagle's. He sat down on the running board of a car across the gravel road and kept on cursing.

Haze walked around the car. Then he looked through the window at the inside of it. Inside it was a dull greenish dust-color. The back seat was missing but it had a two-by-four stretched across the seat frame to sit on. There were dark green fringed window shades on the two side-back windows. He looked through the two front windows and he saw the boy sitting on the running board of the car across the gravel road. He had one trouser leg hitched up and he was scratching his ankle that stuck up out of a pulp of yellow sock. He cursed far down in his throat as if he were trying to get up phlegm. The two window glasses made him a yellow color and distorted his shape. Haze moved quickly from the far side of the car and came around in front. "How much is it?" he asked.

"Jesus on the cross," the boy said, "Christ nailed."

"How much is it?" Haze growled, paling a little.

"How much do you think it's worth?" the boy said. "Give us a estimit."

"It ain't worth what it would take to cart it off. I wouldn't have it."

The boy gave all his attention to his ankle where there was a scab. Haze looked up and saw a man coming from between two cars over on the boy's side. As he came closer, he saw that the man looked exactly like the boy except that he was two heads taller and he had on a sweat-stained brown felt hat. He was coming up behind the boy, between a row of cars. When he got just behind him, he stopped and waited a second. Then he said in a sort of controlled roar, "Get your butt off that running board!"

The boy snarled and disappeared, scrambling between two cars.

The man stood looking at Haze. "What you want?" he asked.

"This car here," Haze said.

"Seventy-fi' dollars," the man said.

On either side of the lot there were two old buildings, reddish with black empty windows, and behind there was another without any windows. "I'm obliged," Haze said, and he started back toward the office.

When he got to the entrance, he glanced back and saw the man about four feet behind him. "We might argue it some," he said.

Haze followed him back to where the car was.

"You won't find a car like that ever' day," the man said. He sat down on the running board that the boy had been sitting on. Haze didn't see the boy but he was there, sitting up on the hood of a car two cars over. He was sitting huddled up as if he were freezing but his face had a sour composed look. "All new tires," the man said.

"They were new when it was built," Haze said.

"They was better cars built a few years ago," the man said. "They don't make no more good cars."

"What you want for it?" Haze asked again.

The man stared off, thinking. After a while he said, "I might could let you have it for sixty-fi'."

Haze leaned against the car and started to roll a cigarette but he couldn't get it rolled. He kept spilling the tobacco and then the papers.

"Well, what you want to pay for it?" the man asked. "I wouldn't trade me a Chrysler for a Essex like that. That car yonder ain't been built by a bunch of niggers.

"All the niggers are living in Detroit now, putting cars together," he said, making conversation. "I was up there a while myself and I seen. I come home."

"I wouldn't pay over thirty dollars for it," Haze said.

"They got one nigger up there," the man said, "is almost

as light as you or me." He took off his hat and ran his finger around the sweat band inside it. He had a little bit of carrot-colored hair.

"We'll drive it around," the man said, "or would you like to get under and look up it?"

"No," Haze said.

The man gave him a half look. "You pay when you leave," he said easily. "You don't find what you looking for in one there's others for the same price obliged to have it." Two cars over the boy began to curse again. It was like a hacking cough. Haze turned suddenly and kicked his foot into the front tire. "I done tole you them tires won't bust," the man said.

"How much?" Haze said.

"I might could make it fifty dollar," the man offered.

Before Haze bought the car, the man put some gas in it and drove him around a few blocks to prove it would run. The boy sat hunched up in the back on the two-by-four, cursing. "Something's wrong with him howcome he curses so much," the man said. "Just don't listen at him." The car rode with a high growling noise. The man put on the brakes to show how well they worked and the boy was thrown off the two-by-four at their heads. "Goddam you," the man roared, "quit jumping at us thataway. Keep your butt on the board." The boy didn't say anything. He didn't even curse. Haze looked back and he was sitting huddled up in the black raincoat with the black leather cap pulled down almost to his eyes. The only thing different was that the ash had been knocked off his cigarette.

He bought the car for forty dollars and then he paid the man extra for five gallons of gasoline. The man had the boy go in the office and bring out a five-gallon can of gas to fill up the tank with. The boy came cursing and lugging the yellow gas can, bent over almost double. "Give it here," Haze said, "I'll do it myself." He was in a terrible hurry to get away in the car. The boy jerked the can away from him and straightened up. It was only half full but he held it over the tank until five gallons would have spilled out slowly. All the time he kept saying, "Sweet Jesus, sweet Jesus, sweet Jesus."

"Why don't he shut up?" Haze said suddenly. "What's he keep talking like that for?"

"I don't never know what ails him," the man said and shrugged.

When the car was ready the man and the boy stood by to watch him drive it off. He didn't want anybody watching him because he hadn't driven a car in four or five years. The man and the boy didn't say anything while he tried to start it. They only stood there, looking in at him. "I wanted this car mostly to be a house for me," he said to the man. "I ain't got any place to be."

"You ain't took the brake off yet," the man said.

He took off the brake and the car shot backward because the man had left it in reverse. In a second he got it going forward and he drove off crookedly, past the man and the boy still standing there watching. He kept going forward, thinking nothing and sweating. For a long time he stayed on the street he was on. He had a hard time holding the car in the road. He went past railroad yards for about a half-mile and then warehouses. When he tried to slow the car down, it stopped altogether and then he had to start it again. He went past long blocks of gray houses and then blocks of better, yellow houses. It began to drizzle rain and he turned on the windshield wipers; they made a great clatter like two idiots clapping in church. He went past blocks of white houses, each sitting with an ugly dog face on a square of grass. Finally he went over a viaduct and found the highway.

He began going very fast.

The highway was ragged with filling stations and trailer camps and roadhouses. After a while there were stretches where red gulleys dropped off on either side of the road and behind them there were patches of field buttoned together with 666 posts. The sky leaked over all of it and then it began to leak into the car. The head of a string of pigs appeared snout-up over the ditch and he had to screech to a stop and watch the rear of the last pig disappear shaking into the ditch on the other side. He started the car again and went on. He had the feeling that everything he saw was a broken-off piece of some giant blank thing that he had forgotten had happened to him. A black pick-up truck turned off a side road in front of him. On the back of it an iron bed and a chair and table were tied, and on top of them, a crate of barred-rock chickens. The truck went very slowly, with a rumbling sound, and in the middle of the road. Haze started pounding his horn and he had hit it three times before he realized it didn't make any sound. The crate was stuffed so full of wet barred-rock chickens that the ones facing him had their heads outside the bars. The truck didn't go any faster and he was forced to drive slowly. The fields stretched sodden on either side until they hit the scrub pines.

The road turned and went down hill and a high em-bankment appeared on one side with pines standing on it, facing a gray boulder that jutted out of the opposite gulley wall. White letters on the boulder said, WOE TO THE BLASPHEMER AND WHOREMONGER! WILL HELL SWALLOW YOU UP? The pick-up truck slowed even more as if it were reading the sign and Haze pounded his empty horn. He beat on it and beat on it but it didn't make any sound. The pick-up truck went on, bumping the glum barred-rock chickens over the edge of the next hill. Haze's car was stopped and his eyes were turned toward the two words at the bottom of the sign. They said in smaller letters, "Jesus Saves."

He sat looking at the sign and he didn't hear the horn. An oil truck as long as a railroad car was behind him. In a second a red square face was at his car window. It watched the back of his neck and hat for a minute and then a hand came in and sat on his shoulder. "What you doing parked in the middle of the road?" the truck driver asked.

Haze turned his fragile placed-looking face toward him. "Take your hand off me," he said. "I'm reading the sign."

The driver's expression and his hand stayed exactly the way they were, as if he didn't hear very well.

"There's no person a whoremonger, who wasn't something worse first," Haze said. "That's not the sin, nor blasphemy. The sin came before them."

The truck driver's face remained exactly the same.

"Jesus is a trick on niggers," Haze said.

The driver put both his hands on the window and gripped it. He looked as if he intended to pick up the car. "Will you get your goddam outhouse off the middle of the road?" he said.

"I don't have to run from anything because I don't believe in anything," Haze said. He and the driver looked at each other for about a minute. Haze's look was the more distant; another plan was forming in his mind. "Which direction is the zoo in?" he asked.

"Back around the other way," the driver said. "Did you exscape from there?"

"I got to see a boy that works in it," Haze said. He started the car up and left the driver standing there, in front of the letters painted on the boulder.

CHAPTER 5

That morning Enoch Emery knew when he woke up that today the person he could show it to was going to come. He knew by his blood. He had wise blood like his daddy.

At two o'clock that afternoon, he greeted the second-shift gate guard. "You ain't but only fifteen minutes late," he said irritably. "But I stayed. I could of went on but I stayed." He wore a green uniform with yellow piping on the neck and sleeves and a yellow stripe down the outside of each leg. The second-shift guard, a boy with a jutting shale-textured face and a toothpick in his mouth, wore the same. The gate they were standing by was made of iron bars and the concrete arch that held it was fashioned to look like two trees; branches curved to form the top of it where twisted letters said, CITY FOREST PARK. The second-shift guard leaned against one of the trunks and began prodding between his teeth with the pick.

"Ever' day," Enoch complained; "look like ever' day I lose fifteen good minutes standing here waiting for you."

Every day when he got off duty, he went into the park, and every day when he went in, he did the same things. He went first to the swimming pool. He was afraid of the water but he liked to sit up on the bank above it if there were any women in the pool, and watch them. There was one woman who came every Monday who wore a bathing suit that was split on each hip. At first he thought she didn't know it, and instead of watching openly on the bank, he had crawled into some bushes, snickering to himself, and had watched from there. There had been no one else in the pool—the crowds didn't come until four o'clock—to tell her about the splits and she had splashed around in the water and then lain up on the edge of the pool asleep for almost an hour, all the time without suspecting there was somebody in the bushes looking at her. Then on another day when he stayed a little later, he saw three women, all with their suits split, the pool full of people, and nobody paying them any mind. That was how the city was—always surprising him. He visited a whore when he felt like it but he was always being shocked by the looseness he saw in the open. He crawled into the bushes out of a sense of propriety. Very often the women would pull the suit straps down off their shoulders and lie stretched out.

The park was the heart of the city. He had come to the city and—with a knowing in his blood—he had established himself at the heart of it. Every day he looked at the heart of it; every day; and he was so stunned and awed and overwhelmed that just to think about it made him sweat. There was something, in the center of the park, that he had discovered. It was a mystery, although it was right there in a glass case for everybody to see and there was a typewritten card over it telling all about it. But there was something the card couldn't say and what it couldn't say was inside him, a terrible knowledge without any words to it, a terrible knowledge like a big nerve growing inside him. He could not show the mystery to just anybody; but he had to show it to somebody. Who he had to show it to was a special person. This person could not be from the city but he didn't know why. He knew he would know him when he saw him and he knew that he would have to see him soon or the nerve inside him would grow so big that he would be forced to steal a car or rob a bank or jump out of a dark alley onto a woman. His blood all morning had been saying the person would come today.

He left the second-shift guard and approached the pool from a discreet footpath that led behind the ladies' end of the bath house to a small clearing where the entire pool could be seen at once. There was nobody in it—the water was bottle-green and motionless—but he saw, coming up the other side and heading for the bath house, the woman with the two little boys. She came every other day or so and brought the two children. She would go in the water with them and swim down the pool and then she would lie up on the side in the sun. She had a stained white bathing suit that fit her like a sack, and Enoch had watched her with pleasure on several occasions. He moved from the clearing up a slope to some abelia bushes. There was a nice tunnel under them and he crawled into it until he came to a slightly wider place where he was accustomed to sit. He settled himself and adjusted the abelia so that he could see through it properly. His face was always very red in the bushes. Anyone who parted the abelia sprigs at just that place, would think he saw a devil and would fall down the slope and into the pool. The woman and the two little boys entered the bath house.

Enoch never went immediately to the dark secret center of the park. That was the peak of the afternoon. The other things he did built up to it. When he left the bushes, he would go to the FROSTY BOTTLE, a hotdog stand in the shape of an Orange Crush with frost painted in blue around the top of it. Here he would have a chocolate malted milkshake and would make some suggestive remarks to the waitress, whom he believed to be secretly in love with him. After that he would go to see the animals. They were in a long set of steel cages like Alcatraz Penitentiary in the movies. The cages were electrically heated in the winter and air-conditioned in the summer and there were six men hired to wait on the animals and feed them T-bone steaks. The animals didn't do anything but lie around. Enoch watched them every day, full of awe and hate. Then he went *there*.

The two little boys ran out the bath house and dived into the water, and simultaneously a grating noise issued from the driveway on the other side of the pool. Enoch's head pierced out of the bushes. He saw a high rat-colored car passing, which sounded as if its motor were dragging out the back. The car passed and he could hear it rattle around the turn in the drive and on away. He listened carefully, trying to hear if it would stop. The noise receded and then gradually grew louder. The car passed again. Enoch saw this time that there was only one person in it, a man. The sound of it died away again and then grew louder. The car came around a third time and stopped almost directly opposite Enoch across the pool. The man in the car looked out the window and down the grass slope to the water where the two little boys were splashing and screaming. Enoch's head was as far out of the bushes as it would come and he was squinting. The door by the man was tied on with a rope. The man got out the other door and walked in front of the car and came halfway down the slope to the pool. He stood there a minute as if he were looking for somebody and then he sat down stiffly on the grass. He had on a blue suit and a black hat. He sat with his knees drawn up. "Well, I'll be dog," Enoch said. "Well, I'll be dog."

He began crawling out of the bushes immediately, his heart moving so fast it was like one of those motorcycles at fairs that the fellow drives around the walls of a pit. He even remembered the man's name—Mr. Hazel Motes. In a second he appeared on all fours at the end of the abelia and looked across the pool. The blue figure was still sitting there in the same position. He had the look of being held there, as if by an invisible hand, as if, if the hand lifted up, the figure would spring across the pool in one leap without the expression on his face changing once.

The woman came out of the bath house and went to the diving board. She spread her arms out and began to bounce, making a big flapping sound with the board. Then suddenly she swirled backward and disappeared below the water. Mr. Hazel Motes's head turned very slowly, following her down the pool.

Enoch got up and went down the path behind the bath house. He came stealthily out on the other side and started walking toward Haze. He stayed on the top of the slope, moving softly in the grass just off the sidewalk, and making no noise. When he was directly behind him, he sat down on the edge of the sidewalk. If his arms had been ten feet long, he could have put his hands on Haze's shoulders. He studied him quietly.

The woman was climbing out of the pool, chinning herself up on the side. First her face appeared, long and cadaverous, with a bandage-like bathing cap coming down almost to her eyes, and sharp teeth protruding from her mouth. Then she rose on her hands until a large foot and leg came up from behind her and another on the other side and she was out, squatting there, panting. She stood up loosely and shook herself, and stamped in the water dripping off her. She was facing them and she grinned. Enoch could see part of Hazel Motes's face watching the woman. It didn't grin in return but it kept on watching her as she padded over to a spot of sun almost directly under where they were sitting. Enoch had to move a little closer to see.

The woman sat down in the spot of sun and took off her bathing cap. Her hair was short and matted and all colors, from deep rust to a greenish yellow. She shook her head and then she looked up at Hazel Motes again, grinning through her pointed teeth. She stretched herself out in the spot of sun, raising her knees and settling her backbone down against the concrete. The two little boys, at the other end of the water, were knocking each other's heads against the side of the pool. She settled herself until she was flat against the concrete and then she reached up and pulled the bathing suit straps off her shoulders.

"King Jesus!" Enoch whispered and before he could get his eyes off the woman, Hazel Motes had sprung up and was almost to his car. The woman was sitting straight up with the suit half off her in front, and Enoch was looking both ways at once.

He wrenched his attention loose from the woman and darted after Hazel Motes. "Wait on me!" he shouted and waved his arms in front of the car which was already rattling and starting to go. Hazel Motes cut off the motor.

His face behind the windshield was sour and frog-like; it looked as if it had a shout closed up in it; it looked like one of those closet doors in gangster pictures where someone is tied to a chair behind it with a towel in his mouth.

"Well," Enoch said, "I declare if it ain't Hazel Motes. How are you, Hazel?"

"The guard said I'd find you at the swimming pool," Hazel Motes said. "He said you hid in the bushes and watched the swimming."

Enoch blushed. "I allus have admired swimming," he said. Then he stuck his head farther through the window. "You were looking for me?" he exclaimed.

"That blind man," Haze said, "that blind man named Hawks—did his child tell you where they lived?"

Enoch didn't seem to hear. "You came out here special to see me?" he said.

"Asa Hawks. His child gave you the peeler. Did she tell you where they lived?"

Enoch eased his head out of the car. He opened the door and climbed in beside Haze. For a minute he only looked at him, wetting his lips. Then he whispered, "I got to show you something."

"I'm looking for those people," Haze said. "I got to see that man. Did she tell you where they lived?"

"I got to show you this thing," Enoch said. "I got to show it to you, here, this afternoon. I got to." He gripped Hazel Motes's arm and Haze shook him off.

"Did she tell you where they live?" he said again.

Enoch kept wetting his lips. They were pale except for his fever blister, which was purple. "Cert'nly," he said. "Ain't she invited me to come to see her and bring my mouth organ? I got to show you this thing, then I'll tell you."

"What thing?" Haze muttered.

"This thing I got to show you," Enoch said. "Drive straight on ahead and I'll tell you where to stop."

"I don't want to see anything of yours," Haze Motes said. "I want that address."

Enoch didn't look at Hazel Motes. He looked out the window. "I won't be able to remember it unless you come," he said. In a minute the car started. Enoch's blood was beating fast. He knew he had to go to the FROSTY BOTTLE and the zoo before there, and he foresaw a terrible struggle with Hazel Motes. He would have to get him there, even if he had to hit him over the head with a rock and carry him on his back up to it.

Enoch's brain was divided into two parts. The part in communication with his blood did the figuring but it never said anything in words. The other part was stocked up with all kinds of words and phrases. While the first part was figuring how to get Hazel Motes through the FROSTY BOTTLE and the zoo, the second inquired, "Where'd you git thisyer fine car? You ought to paint you some signs on the outside it, like 'Step-in, baby'—I seen one with that on it, then I seen another, said . . ."

Hazel Motes's face might have been cut out of the side of a rock.

"My daddy once owned a yeller Ford automobile he won on a ticket," Enoch murmured. "It had a roll-top and two aerials and a squirrel tail all come with it. He swapped it off. Stop here! Stop here!" he yelled—they were passing the FROSTY BOTTLE.

"Where is it?" Hazel Motes said as soon as they were inside. They were in a dark room with a counter across the back of it and brown stools like toad stools in front of the counter. On the wall facing the door there was a large advertisement for ice cream, showing a cow dressed up like a housewife.

"It ain't here," Enoch said. "We have to stop here on the way and get something to eat. What you want?"

"Nothing," Haze said. He stood stiffly in the middle of the room with his hands in his pockets.

"Well, sit down," Enoch said. "I have to have a little drink."

Something stirred behind the counter and a woman with bobbed hair like a man's got up from a chair where she had been reading the newspaper, and came forward. She looked sourly at Enoch. She had on a once-white uniform clotted with brown stains. "What you want?" she said in a loud voice, leaning close to his ear. She had a man's face and big muscled arms.

"I want a chocolate malted milkshake, baby girl," Enoch said softly. "I want a lot of ice cream in it."

She turned fiercely from him and glared at Haze.

"He says he don't want nothing but to sit down and look at you for a while," Enoch said. "He ain't hungry but for just to see you."

Haze looked woodenly at the woman and she turned her back on him and began mixing the milkshake. He sat down on the last stool in the row and started cracking his knuckles.

Enoch watched him carefully. "I reckon you done changed some," he said after a few minutes.

Haze got up. "Give me those people's address. Right now," he said.

It came to Enoch in an instant—the police. His face was suddenly suffused with secret knowledge. "I reckon you ain't as uppity as you was last night," he said. "I reckon maybe," he said, "you ain't got so much cause now as you had then." Stole theter automobile, he thought.

Hazel Motes sat back down.

"Howcome you jumped up so fast down yonder by the pool?" Enoch asked. The woman turned around to him with the malted milk in her hand. "Of course," he said evilly, "I wouldn't have had no truck with a ugly dish like that neither."

The woman thumped the malted milk on the counter in front of him. "Fifteen cents," she roared.

"You're worth more than that, baby girl," Enoch said. He snickered and began gassing his malted milk through the straw.

The woman strode over to where Haze was. "What you come in here with a son of a bitch like that for?" she shouted. "A nice quiet boy like you to come in here with a son of a bitch. You ought to mind the company you keep." Her name was Maude and she drank whisky all day from a fruit jar under the counter. "Jesus," she said, wiping her hand under her nose. She sat down in a straight chair in front of Haze but facing Enoch, and folded her arms across her chest. "Ever' day," she said to Haze, looking at Enoch, "ever' day that son of a bitch comes in here."

Enoch was thinking about the animals. They had to go next to see the animals. He hated them; just thinking about them made his face turn a chocolate purple color as if the malted milk were rising in his head.

"You're a nice boy," she said. "I can see, you got a clean nose, well keep it clean, don't go messin' with a son a bitch like that yonder. I always know a clean boy when I see one." She was shouting at Enoch, but Enoch watched Hazel Motes. It was as if something inside Hazel Motes was winding up, although he didn't move on the outside. He only looked pressed down in that blue suit, as if inside it, the thing winding was getting tighter and tighter.

Enoch's blood told him to hurry. He raced the milkshake up the straw.

"Yes sir," she said, "there ain't anything sweeter than a clean boy. God for my witness. And I know a clean one when I see him and I know a son a bitch when I see him and there's a heap of difference and that pus-marked bastard zlurping through that straw is a goddamned son a bitch and you a clean boy had better mind how you keep him company. I know a clean boy when I see one."

Enoch screeched in the bottom of his glass. He fished fifteen cents from his pocket and laid it on the counter and got up. But Hazel Motes was already up; he was leaning over the counter toward the woman. She didn't see him right away because she was looking at Enoch. He leaned on his hands over the counter until his face was just a foot from hers. She turned around and stared at him.

"Come on," Enoch started, "we don't have no time to be sassing around with her. I got to show you this right away, I got . . ."

"I AM clean," Haze said.

It was not until he said it again that Enoch caught the words.

"I AM clean," he said again, without any expression on his face or in his voice, just looking at the woman as if he were looking at a wall. "If Jesus existed, I wouldn't be clean," he said.

She stared at him, startled and then outraged. "What do

you think I care!" she yelled. "Why should I give a goddam what you are!"

"Come on," Enoch whined, "come on or I won't tell you where them people live." He caught Haze's arm and pulled him back from the counter and toward the door.

"You bastard!" the woman screamed, "what do you think I care about any of you filthy boys?"

Hazel Motes pushed the door open quickly and went out. He got back in his car and Enoch climbed in behind him. "Okay," Enoch said, "drive straight on ahead down this road."

"What you want for telling me?" Haze said. "I'm not staying here. I have to go. I can't stay here any longer."

Enoch shuddered. He began wetting his lips. "I got to show it to you," he said hoarsely. "I can't show it to nobody but you. I had a sign it was you when I seen you drive up at the pool. I knew all morning somebody was going to come and then when I saw you at the pool, I had thisyer sign."

"I don't care about your signs," Haze said.

"I go to see it ever' day," Enoch said. "I go ever' day but I ain't ever been able to take nobody else with me. I had to wait on the sign. I'll tell you them people's address just as soon as you see it. You got to see it," he said. "When you see it, something's going to happen."

"Nothing's going to happen," Haze said.

He started the car again and Enoch sat forward on the

seat. "Them animals," he muttered. "We got to walk by them first. It won't take long for that. It won't take a minute." He saw the animals waiting evil-eyed for him, ready to throw him off time. He thought what if the police were screaming out here now with sirens and squad cars and they got Hazel Motes just before he showed it to him.

"I got to see those people," Haze said.

"Stop here! Stop here!" Enoch yelled.

There was a long shining row of steel cages over to the left and behind the bars, black shapes were sitting or pacing. "Get out," Enoch said. "This won't take one second."

Haze got out. Then he stopped. "I got to see those people," he said.

"Okay, okay, come on," Enoch whined.

"I don't believe you know the address."

"I do! I do!" Enoch cried. "It begins with a three, now come on!" He pulled Haze toward the cages. Two black bears sat in the first one, facing each other like two matrons having tea, their faces polite and self-absorbed. "They don't do nothing but sit there all day and stink," Enoch said. "A man comes and washes them cages out ever' morning with a hose and it stinks just as much as if he'd left it." He went past two more cages of bears, not looking at them, and then he stopped at the next cage where there were two yellow-eyed wolves nosing around the edges of the concrete. "Hyenas," he said. "I ain't got no use for hyenas." He leaned closer and spit into the cage, hitting one of the wolves on the leg. It shuttled to the side, giving him a slanted evil look. For a second he forgot Hazel Motes. Then he looked back quickly to make sure he was still there. He was right behind him. He was not looking at the animals. Thinking about them police, Enoch thought. He said, "Come on, we don't have time to look at all theseyer monkeys that come next." Usually he stopped at every cage and made an obscene comment aloud to himself, but today the animals were only a form he had to get through. He hurried past the cages of monkeys, looking back two or three times to make sure Hazel Motes was behind him. At the last of the monkey cages, he stopped as if he couldn't help himself.

"Look at that ape," he said, glaring. The animal had its back to him, gray except for a small pink seat. "If I had a ass like that," he said prudishly, "I'd sit on it. I wouldn't be exposing it to all these people come to this park. Come on, we don't have to look at theseyer birds that come next." He ran past the cages of birds and then he was at the end of the zoo. "Now we don't need the car," he said, going on ahead, "we'll go right down that hill yonder through them trees." Haze had stopped at the last cage for birds. "Oh Jesus," Enoch groaned. He stood and waved his arms wildly and shouted, "Come on!" but Haze didn't move from where he was looking into the cage.

Enoch ran back to him and grabbed him by the arm but Haze pushed him off and kept on looking in the cage. It was empty. Enoch stared. "It's empty!" he shouted. "What you have to look in that ole empty cage for? You come on!" He stood there, sweating and purple. "It's empty!" he shouted. And then he saw it wasn't empty. Over in one corner on the floor of the cage, there was an eye. The eye was in the middle of something that looked like a piece of mop sitting on an old rag. He squinted close to the wire and saw that the piece of mop was an owl with one eye open. It was looking directly at Hazel Motes. "That ain't nothing but a ole hoot owl," he moaned. "You seen them things before."

"I AM clean," Haze said to the eye. He said it just the way he said it to the woman in the FROSTY BOTTLE. The eye shut softly and the owl turned its face to the wall.

He's done murdered somebody, Enoch thought. "Oh sweet Jesus, come on!" he wailed. "I got to show you this right now." He pulled him away but a few feet from the cage, Haze stopped again, looking at something in the distance. Enoch's eyesight was very poor. He squinted and made out a figure far down the road behind them. There were two smaller figures jumping on either side of it.

Hazel Motes turned back to him suddenly and said, "Where's this thing? Let's see it right now and get it over with. Come on."

"Ain't that where I been trying to take you?" Enoch said. He felt the perspiration drying on him and stinging and his skin was pin-pointed, even in his scalp. "We got to cross this road and go down this hill. We got to go on foot," he said.

"Why?" Haze muttered.

"I don't know," Enoch said. He knew something was going to happen to him. His blood stopped beating. All the time it had been beating like drum noises and now it had stopped. They started down the hill. It was a steep hill, full of trees painted white from the ground up four feet. They looked as if they had on ankle-socks. He gripped Hazel Motes's arm. "It gets damp as you go down," he said, looking around vaguely. Hazel Motes shook him off. In a second, Enoch gripped his arm again and stopped him. He pointed down through the trees. "Muvseevum," he said. The strange word made him shiver. That was the first time he had ever said it aloud. A piece of gray building was showing where he pointed. It grew larger as they went down the hill, then as they came to the end of the wood and stepped out on the gravel driveway, it seemed to shrink suddenly. It was round and soot-colored. There were columns at the front of it and in between each column there was an eyeless stone woman holding a pot on her head. A concrete band was over the columns and the letters, M V S E V M, were cut into it. Enoch was afraid to pronounce the word again.

"We got to go up the steps and through the front door," he whispered. There were ten steps up to the porch. The door was wide and black. Enoch pushed it in cautiously and inserted his head in the crack. In a minute he brought it out again and said, "All right, go on in and walk easy. I don't want to wake up theter ole guard. He ain't very friendly with me." They went into a dark hall. It was heavy with the odor of linoleum and creosote and another odor behind these two. The third one was an undersmell and Enoch couldn't name it as anything he had ever smelled before. There was nothing in the hall but two urns and an old man asleep in a straight chair against the wall. He had on the same kind of uniform as Enoch and he looked like a dried-up spider stuck there. Enoch looked at Hazel Motes to see if he was smelling the undersmell. He looked as if he were. Enoch's blood began to beat again, urging him forward. He gripped Haze's arm and tiptoed through the hall to another black door at the end of it. He cracked it a little and inserted his head in the crack. Then in a second he drew it out and crooked his finger in a gesture for Haze to follow him. They went into another hall, like the last one, but running crosswise. "It's in that first door yonder," Enoch said in a small voice. They went into a dark room full of glass cases. The glass cases covered the walls and there were three coffin-like ones in the middle of the floor. The ones on the walls were full of birds tilted on varnished sticks and looking down with dried piquant expressions.

"Come on," Enoch whispered. He went past the two cases in the middle of the floor and toward the third one.

He went to the farthest end of it and stopped. He stood looking down with his neck thrust forward and his hands clutched together; Hazel Motes moved up beside him.

The two of them stood there, Enoch rigid and Hazel Motes bent slightly forward. There were three bowls and a row of blunt weapons and a man in the case. It was the man Enoch was looking at. He was about three feet long. He was naked and a dried yellow color and his eyes were drawn almost shut as if a giant block of steel were falling down on top of him.

"See theter notice," Enoch said in a church whisper, pointing to a typewritten card at the man's foot, "it says he was once as tall as you or me. Some A-rabs did it to him in six months." He turned his head cautiously to see Hazel Motes.

All he could tell was that Hazel Motes's eyes were on the shrunken man. He was bent forward so that his face was reflected on the glass top of the case. The reflection was pale and the eyes were like two clean bullet holes. Enoch waited, rigid. He heard footsteps in the hall. Oh Jesus Jesus, he prayed, let him hurry up and do whatever he's going to do! The woman with the two little boys came in the door. She had one by each hand, and she was grinning. Hazel Motes had not raised his eyes once from the shrunken man. The woman came toward them. She stopped on the other side of the case and looked down into it and the

94

reflection of her face appeared grinning on the glass, over Hazel Motes's.

She snickered and put two fingers in front of her teeth. The little boys' faces were like pans set on either side to catch the grins that overflowed from her. When Haze saw her face on the glass, his neck jerked back and he made a noise. It might have come from the man inside the case. In a second Enoch knew it had. "Wait!" he screamed, and tore out of the room after Hazel Motes.

He overtook him halfway up the hill. He caught him by the arm and swung him around and then he stood there, suddenly weak and light as a balloon, and stared. Hazel Motes grabbed him by the shoulders and shook him. "What is that address!" he shouted. "Give me that address!"

Even if Enoch had been sure what the address was, he couldn't have thought of it then. He could not even stand up. As soon as Hazel Motes let him go, he fell backward and landed against one of the white-socked trees. He rolled over and lay stretched out on the ground, with an exalted look on his face. He thought he was floating. A long way off he saw the blue figure spring and pick up a rock, and he saw the wild face turn, and the rock hurtle toward him; he shut his eyes tight and the rock hit him on the forehead.

When he came to again, Hazel Motes was gone. He lay there a minute. He put his fingers to his forehead and then held them in front of his eyes. They were streaked with red. He turned his head and saw a drop of blood on the ground and as he looked at it, he thought it widened like a little spring. He sat straight up, frozen-skinned, and put his finger in it, and very faintly he could hear his blood beating, his secret blood, in the center of the city.

Then he knew that whatever was expected of him was only just beginning.

CHAPTER 6

That evening Haze drove his car around the streets until he found the blind man and the child again. They were standing on a corner, waiting for the light to change. He drove the Essex at some distance behind them for about four blocks up the main street and then turned it after them down a side street. He followed them on into a dark section past the railroad yards and watched them go up on the porch of a box-like two-story house. When the blind man opened the door a shaft of light fell on him and Haze craned his neck to see him better. The child turned her head, slowly, as if it worked on a screw, and watched his car pass. His face was so close to the glass that it looked like a paper face pasted there. He noted the number of the house and a sign on it that said, ROOMS FOR RENT.

Then he drove back down town and parked the Essex in front of a movie house where he could catch the drain of people coming out from the picture show. The lights around the marquee were so bright that the moon, mov-

99

ing overhead with a small procession of clouds behind it, looked pale and insignificant. Haze got out of the Essex and climbed up on the nose of it.

A thin little man with a long upper lip was at the glass ticket box, buying tickets for three portly women who were behind him. "Gotta get these girls some refreshments too," he said to the woman in the ticket box. "Can't have 'em starve right before my eyes."

"Ain't he a card?" one of the women hollered. "He keeps me in stitches!"

Three boys in red satin lumberjackets came out of the foyer. Haze raised his arms. "Where has the blood you think you been redeemed by touched you?" he cried.

The women all turned around at once and stared at him.

"A wise guy," the little thin man said, and glared as if someone were about to insult him.

The three boys moved up, pushing each other's shoulders.

Haze waited a second and then he cried again. "Where has the blood you think you been redeemed by touched you?"

"Rabble rouser," the little man said. "One thing I can't stand it's a rabble rouser."

"What church you belong to, you boy there?" Haze asked, pointing at the tallest boy in the red satin lumberjacket.

The boy giggled.

"You then," he said impatiently, pointing at the next one. "What church you belong to?"

"Church of Christ," the boy said in a falsetto to hide the truth.

"Church of Christ!" Haze repeated. "Well, I preach the Church Without Christ. I'm member and preacher to that church where the blind don't see and the lame don't walk and what's dead stays that way. Ask me about that church and I'll tell you it's the church that the blood of Jesus don't foul with redemption."

"He's a preacher," one of the women said. "Let's go."

"Listen, you people, I'm going to take the truth with me wherever I go," Haze called. "I'm going to preach it to whoever'll listen at whatever place. I'm going to preach there was no Fall because there was nothing to fall from and no Redemption because there was no Fall and no Judgment because there wasn't the first two. Nothing matters but that Jesus was a liar."

The little man herded his girls into the picture show quickly and the three boys left but more people came out and he began over and said the same thing again. They left and some more came and he said it a third time. Then they left and no one else came out; there was no one there but the woman in the glass box. She had been glaring at him all the time but he had not noticed her. She wore glasses with rhinestones in the bows and she had white hair stacked in sausages around her head. She stuck her mouth to a hole in the glass and shouted, "Listen, if you don't have a church to do it in, you don't have to do it in front of this show."

"My church is the Church Without Christ, lady," he said. "If there's no Christ, there's no reason to have a set place to do it in."

"Listen," she said, "if you don't get from in front of this show, I'll call the police."

"There's plenty of shows," he said and got down and got back in the Essex and drove off. That night he preached in front of three other picture shows before he went to Mrs. Watts.

In the morning he drove back to the house where the blind man and the child had gone in the night before. It was yellow clapboard, the second one in a block of them, all alike. He went up to the front door and rang the bell. After a few minutes a woman with a mop opened it. He said he wanted to rent a room.

"What you do?" she asked. She was a tall bony woman, resembling the mop she carried upside-down.

He said he was a preacher.

The woman looked at him thoroughly and then she looked behind him at his car. "What church?" she asked.

He said the Church Without Christ.

"Protestant?" she asked suspiciously, "or something foreign?"

He said no mam, it was Protestant.

After a minute she said, "Well, you can look at it," and he followed her into a white plastered hall and up some steps at the side of it. She opened a door into a back room that was a little larger than his car, with a cot and a chest of drawers and a table and straight chair in it. There were two nails on the wall to hang clothes on. "Three dollars a week in advance," she said. There was one window and another door opposite the door they had come in by. Haze opened the extra door, expecting it to be a closet. It opened out onto a drop of about thirty feet and looked down into a narrow bare back yard where the garbage was collected. There was a plank nailed across the door frame at knee level to keep anyone from falling out. "A man named Hawks lives here, don't he?" Haze asked quickly.

"Downstairs in the front room," she said, "him and his child." She was looking down into the drop too. "It used to be a fire-escape there," she said, "but I don't know what happened to it."

He paid her three dollars and took possession of the room, and as soon as she was out of the way, he went down the stairs and knocked on the Hawkses' door.

The blind man's child opened it a crack and stood looking at him. She seemed at once to have to balance her face so that her expression would be the same on both sides. "It's that boy, Papa," she said in a low tone. "The one that keeps following me." She held the door close to her head so he couldn't see in past her. The blind man came to the door but he didn't open it any wider. His look was not the same as it had been two nights before; it was sour and unfriendly, and he didn't speak, he only stood there.

Haze had got what he had to say in mind before he left his room. "I live here," he said. "I thought if your girl wanted to give me so much eye, I might return her some of it." He wasn't looking at the girl; he was staring at the black glasses and the curious scars that started somewhere behind them and ran down the blind man's cheeks.

"What I give you the other night," she said, "was a looker indignation for what I seen you do. It was you give me the eye. You should have seen him, Papa," she said, "looked me up and down."

"I've started my own church," Haze said. "The Church Without Christ. I preach on the street."

"You can't let me alone, can you?" Hawks said. His voice was flat, nothing like it had been the other time. "I didn't ask you to come here and I ain't asking you to hang around," he said.

Haze had expected a secret welcome. He waited, trying to think of something to say. "What kind of a preacher are you?" he heard himself murmur, "not to see if you can save my soul?" The blind man pushed the door shut in his face. Haze stood there a second facing the blank door, and then he ran his sleeve across his mouth and went out.

Inside, Hawks took off his dark glasses and, from a hole in the window shade, watched him get in his car and drive off. The eye he put to the hole was slightly rounder and smaller than his other one, but it was obvious he could see out of both of them. The child watched from a lower crack. "Howcome you don't like him, Papa?" she asked, "—because he's after me?"

"If he was after you, that would be enough to make me welcome him," he said.

"I like his eyes," she observed. "They don't look like they see what he's looking at but they keep on looking."

Their room was the same size as Haze's but there were two cots and an oil cooking stove and a wash basin in it and a trunk that they used for a table. Hawks sat down on one of the cots and put a cigarette in his mouth. "Goddam Jesus-hog," he muttered.

"Well, look what you used to be," she said. "Look what you tried to do. You got over it and so will he."

"I don't want him hanging around," he said. "He makes me nervous."

"Listen here," she said, sitting down on the cot with him, "you help me to get him and then you go away and do what you please and I can live with him."

"He don't even know you exist," Hawks said.

"Even if he don't," she said, "that's all right. That's howcome I can get him easy. I want him and you ought to help and then you could go on off like you want to."

He lay down on the cot and finished the cigarette; his face was thoughtful and evil. Once while he was lying there, he laughed and then his expression constricted again. "Well, that might be fine," he said after a while. "That might be the oil on Aaron's beard."

"Listen here," she said, "it would be the nuts! I'm just crazy about him. I never seen a boy that I liked the looks of any better. Don't run him off. Tell him how you blinded yourself for Jesus and show him that clipping you got."

"Yeah, the clipping," he said.

Haze had gone out in his car to think and he had decided that he would seduce Hawks's child. He thought that when the blind preacher saw his daughter ruined, he would realize that he was in earnest when he said he preached The Church Without Christ. Besides this reason, there was another: he didn't want to go back to Mrs. Watts. The night before, after he was asleep, she had got up and cut the top of his hat out in an obscene shape. He felt that he should have a woman, not for the sake of the pleasure in her, but to prove that he didn't believe in sin since he practiced what was called it; but he had had enough of her. He wanted someone he could teach something to and he took it for granted that the blind man's child, since she was so homely, would also be innocent.

Before he went back to his room, he went to a dry-goods store to buy a new hat. He wanted one that was completely opposite to the old one. This time he was sold a white panama with a red and green and yellow band around it.

The man said they were really the thing and particularly if he was going to Florida.

"I ain't going to Florida," he said. "This hat is opposite from the one I used to have is all."

"You can use it anywheres," the man said; "it's new."

"I know that," Haze said. He went outside and took the red and green and yellow band off it and thumped out the crease in the top and turned down the brim. When he put it on, it looked just as fierce as the other one had.

He didn't go back to the Hawkses' door until late in the afternoon, when he thought they would be eating their supper. It opened almost at once and the child's head appeared in the crack. He pushed the door out of her hand and went in without looking at her directly. Hawks was sitting at the trunk. The remains of his supper were in front of him but he wasn't eating. He had barely got the black glasses on in time.

"If Jesus cured blind men, howcome you don't get Him to cure you?" Haze asked. He had prepared this sentence in his room.

"He blinded Paul," Hawks said.

Haze sat down on the edge of one of the cots. He looked around him and then back at Hawks. He crossed and uncrossed his knees and then he crossed them again. "Where'd you get them scars?" he asked.

The fake blind man leaned forward and smiled. "You

still have a chance to save yourself if you repent," he said. "I can't save you but you can save yourself."

"That's what I've already done," Haze said. "Without the repenting. I preach how I done it every night on the . . ."

"Look at this," Hawks said. He took a yellow newspaper clipping from his pocket and handed it to him, and his mouth twisted out of the smile. "This is how I got the scars," he muttered. The child made a sign to him from the door to smile and not look sour. As he waited for Haze to finish reading, the smile slowly returned.

The headline on the clipping said, EVANGELIST PROMISES TO BLIND SELF. The rest of it said that Asa Hawks, an evangelist of the Free Church of Christ, had promised to blind himself to justify his belief that Christ Jesus had redeemed him. It said he would do it at a revival on Saturday night at eight o'clock, the fourth of October. The date on it was more than ten years before. Over the headline was a picture of Hawks, a scarless, straight-mouthed man of about thirty, with one eye a little smaller and rounder than the other. The mouth had a look that might have been either holy or calculating, but there was a wildness in the eyes that suggested terror.

Haze sat staring at the clipping after he had read it. He read it three times. He took his hat off and put it on again and got up and stood looking around the room as if he were trying to remember where the door was.

"He did it with lime," the child said, "and there was hundreds converted. Anybody that blinded himself for justification ought to be able to save you—or even somebody of his blood," she added, inspired.

"Nobody with a good car needs to be justified," Haze murmured. He scowled at her and hurried out the door, but as soon as it was shut behind him, he remembered something. He turned around and opened it and handed her a piece of paper, folded up several times into a small pellet shape; then he hurried out to his car.

Hawks took the note away from her and opened it up. It said, Babe, I never saw anybody that looked as good as you before is why I came here. She read it over his arm, coloring pleasantly.

"Now you got the written proof for it, Papa," she said.

"That bastard got away with my clipping," Hawks muttered.

"Well you got another clipping, ain't you?" she asked, with a little smirk.

"Shut your mouth," he said and flung himself down on the cot. The other clipping was one that said, Evangelist's nerve fails.

"I can get it for you," she offered, standing close to the door so that she could run if she disturbed him too much, but he had turned toward the wall as if he were going to sleep.

Ten years ago at a revival he had intended to blind

109

himself and two hundred people or more were there, waiting for him to do it. He had preached for an hour on the blindness of Paul, working himself up until he saw himself struck blind by a Divine flash of lightning and, with courage enough then, he had thrust his hands into the bucket of wet lime and streaked them down his face; but he hadn't been able to let any of it get into his eyes. He had been possessed of as many devils as were necessary to do it, but at that instant, they disappeared, and he saw himself standing there as he was. He fancied Jesus, Who had expelled them, was standing there too, beckoning to him; and he had fled out of the tent into the alley and disappeared.

"Okay, Pa," she said, "I'll go out for a while and leave you in peace."

Haze had driven his car immediately to the nearest garage where a man with black bangs and a short expressionless face had come out to wait on him. He told the man he wanted the horn made to blow and the leaks taken out of the gas tank, the starter made to work smoother and the windshield wipers tightened.

The man lifted the hood and glanced inside and then shut it again. Then he walked around the car, stopping to lean on it here and there, and thumping it in one place and another. Haze asked him how long it would take to put it in the best order.

"It can't be done," the man said.

"This is a good car," Haze said. "I knew when I first saw it that it was the car for me, and since I've had it, I've had a place to be that I can always get away in."

"Was you going some place in this?" the man asked.

"To another garage," Haze said, and he got in the Essex and drove off. At the other garage he went to, there was a man who said he could put the car in the best shape overnight, because it was such a good car to begin with, so well put together and with such good materials in it, and because, he added, he was the best mechanic in town, working in the best-equipped shop. Haze left it with him, certain that it was in honest hands.

CHAPTER 7

The next afternoon when he got his car back, he drove it out into the country to see how well it worked on the open road. The sky was just a little lighter blue than his suit, clear and even, with only one cloud in it, a large blinding white one with curls and a beard. He had gone about a mile out of town when he heard a throat cleared behind him. He slowed down and turned his head and saw Hawks's child getting up off the floor onto the two-by-four that stretched across the seat frame. "I been here all the time," she said, "and you never known it." She had a bunch of dandelions in her hair and a wide red mouth on her pale face.

"What do you want to hide in my car for?" he said angrily. "I got business before me. I don't have time for foolishness." Then he checked his ugly tone and stretched his mouth a little, remembering that he was going to seduce her. "Yeah sure," he said, "glad to see you."

She swung one thin black-stockinged leg over the back

of the front seat and then let the rest of herself over. "Did you mean 'good to look at' in that note, or only 'good'?" she asked.

"The both," he said stiffly.

"My name is Sabbath," she said. "Sabbath Lily Hawks. My mother named me that just after I was born because I was born on the Sabbath and then she turned over in her bed and died and I never seen her."

"Unh," Haze said. His jaw tightened and he entrenched himself behind it and drove on. He had not wanted any company. His sense of pleasure in the car and in the afternoon was gone.

"Him and her wasn't married," she continued, "and that makes me a bastard, but I can't help it. It was what he done to me and not what I done to myself."

"A bastard?" he murmured. He couldn't see how a preacher who had blinded himself for Jesus could have a bastard. He turned his head and looked at her with interest for the first time.

She nodded and the corners of her mouth turned up. "A real bastard," she said, catching his elbow, "and do you know what? A bastard shall not enter the kingdom of heaven!" she said.

Haze was driving his car toward the ditch while he stared at her. "How could you be . . . ," he started and saw the red embankment in front of him and pulled the car back on the road.

"Do you read the papers?" she asked.

"No," he said.

"Well, there's this woman in it named Mary Brittle that tells you what to do when you don't know. I wrote her a letter and ast her what I was to do."

"How could you be a bastard when he blinded him . . . ," he started again.

"I says, 'Dear Mary, I am a bastard and a bastard shall not enter the kingdom of heaven as we all know, but I have this personality that makes boys follow me. Do you think I should neck or not? I shall not enter the kingdom of heaven anyway so I don't see what difference it makes.'"

"Listen here," Haze said, "if he blinded himself how . . ."

"Then she answered my letter in the paper. She said, 'Dear Sabbath, Light necking is acceptable, but I think your real problem is one of adjustment to the modern world. Perhaps you ought to re-examine your religious values to see if they meet your needs in Life. A religious experience can be a beautiful addition to living if you put it in the proper prespective and do not let it warf you. Read some books on Ethical Culture.'"

"You couldn't be a bastard," Haze said, getting very pale. "You must be mixed up. Your daddy blinded himself."

"Then I wrote her another letter," she said, scratching his ankle with the toe of her sneaker, and smiling, "I says, 'Dear Mary, What I really want to know is should I go the whole hog or not? That's my real problem. I'm adjusted okay to the modern world.' "

"Your daddy blinded himself," Haze repeated.

"He wasn't always as good as he is now," she said. "She never answered my second letter."

"You mean in his youth he didn't believe but he came to?" he asked. "Is that what you mean or ain't it?" and he kicked her foot roughly away from his.

"That's right," she said. Then she drew herself up a little. "Quit that feeling my leg with yours," she said.

The blinding white cloud was a little ahead of them, moving to the left. "Why don't you turn down that dirt road?" she asked. The highway forked off onto a clay road and he turned onto it. It was hilly and shady and the country showed to advantage on either side. One side was dense honeysuckle and the other was open and slanted down to a telescoped view of the city. The white cloud was directly in front of them.

"How did he come to believe?" Haze asked. "What changed him into a preacher for Jesus?"

"I do like a dirt road," she said, "particularly when it's hilly like this one here. Why don't we get out and sit under a tree where we could get better acquainted?"

After a few hundred feet Haze stopped the car and they got out. "Was he a very evil-seeming man before he came to believe," he asked, "or just part way evil-seeming?"

"All the way evil," she said, going under the barbed wire

fence on the side of the road. Once under it she sat down and began to take off her shoes and stockings. "How I like to walk in a field is barefooted," she said with gusto.

"Listenhere," Haze muttered, "I got to be going back to town. I don't have time to walk in any field," but he went under the fence and on the other side he said, "I suppose before he came to believe he didn't believe at all."

"Let's us go over that hill yonder and sit under the trees," she said.

They climbed the hill and went down the other side of it, she a little ahead of Haze. He saw that sitting under a tree with her might help him to seduce her, but he was in no hurry to get on with it, considering her innocence. He felt it was too hard a job to be done in an afternoon. She sat down under a large pine and patted the ground close beside her for him to sit on, but he sat about five feet away from her on a rock. He rested his chin on his knees and looked straight ahead.

"I can save you," she said. "I got a church in my heart where Jesus is King."

He leaned in her direction, glaring. "I believe in a new kind of jesus," he said, "one that can't waste his blood redeeming people with it, because he's all man and ain't got any God in him. My church is the Church Without Christ!"

She moved up closer to him. "Can a bastard be saved in it?" she asked.

"There's no such thing as a bastard in the Church Without Christ," he said. "Everything is all one. A bastard wouldn't be any different from anybody else."

"That's good," she said.

He looked at her irritably, for something in his mind was already contradicting him and saying that a bastard couldn't, that there was only one truth—that Jesus was a liar—and that her case was hopeless. She pulled open her collar and lay down on the ground full length. "Ain't my feet white, though?" she asked raising them slightly.

Haze didn't look at her feet. The thing in his mind said that the truth didn't contradict itself and that a bastard couldn't be saved in the Church Without Christ. He decided he would forget it, that it was not important.

"There was this child once," she said, turning over on her stomach, "that nobody cared if it lived or died. Its kin sent it around from one to another of them and finally to its grandmother who was a very evil woman and she couldn't stand to have it around because the least good thing made her break out in these welps. She would get all itching and swoll. Even her eyes would itch her and swell up and there wasn't nothing she could do but run up and down the road, shaking her hands and cursing and it was twicet as bad when this child was there so she kept the child locked up in a chicken crate. It seen its granny in hell-fire, swoll and burning, and it told her everything it seen and she got so swoll until finally she went to the well and wrapped the well rope around her neck and let down the bucket and broke her neck.

"Would you guess me to be fifteen years old?" she asked.

"There wouldn't be any sense to the word, bastard, in the Church Without Christ," Haze said.

"Why don't you lie down and rest yourself?" she inquired.

Haze moved a few feet away and lay down. He put his hat over his face and folded his arms across his chest. She lifted herself up on her hands and knees and crawled over to him and gazed at the top of his hat. Then she lifted it off like a lid and peered into his eyes. They stared straight upward. "It don't make any difference to me," she said softly, "how much you like me."

He trained his eyes into her neck. Gradually she lowered her head until the tips of their noses almost touched but still he didn't look at her. "I see you," she said in a playful voice.

"Git away!" he said, jumping violently.

She scrambled up and ran around behind the tree. Haze put his hat back on and stood up, shaken. He wanted to get back in the Essex. He realized suddenly that it was parked on a country road, unlocked, and that the first person passing would drive off in it.

"I see you," a voice said from behind the tree.

He walked off quickly in the opposite direction toward

the car. The jubilant expression on the face that looked from around the tree, flattened.

He got in his car and went through the motions of starting it but it only made a noise like water lost somewhere in the pipes. A panic took him and he began to pound the starter. There were two instruments on the dashboard with needles that pointed dizzily in first one direction and then another, but they worked on a private system, independent of the whole car. He couldn't tell if it was out of gas or not. Sabbath Hawks came running up to the fence. She got down on the ground and rolled under the barbed wire and then stood at the window of the car, looking in at him. He turned his head at her fiercely and said, "What did you do to my car?" Then he got out and started walking down the road, without waiting for her to answer. After a second, she followed him, keeping her distance.

Where the highway had forked off onto the dirt road, there had been a store with a gas pump in front of it. It was about a half-mile back; Haze kept up a steady fast pace until he reached it. It had a deserted look, but after a few minutes a man appeared from out of the woods behind it, and Haze told him what he wanted. While the man got out his pick-up truck to drive them back to the Essex, Sabbath Hawks arrived and went over to a cage about six feet high that was at the side of the shack. Haze had not noticed it until she came up. He saw that there was something alive

in it, and went near enough to read a sign that said, TWO
DEADLY ENEMIES. HAVE A LOOK FREE.

There was a black bear about four feet long and very
thin, resting on the floor of the cage; his back was spotted
with bird lime that had been shot down on him by a small
chicken hawk that was sitting on a perch in the upper part
of the same apartment. Most of the hawk's tail was gone;
the bear had only one eye.

"Come on here if you don't want to get left," Haze said
roughly, grabbing her by the arm. The man had his truck
ready and the three of them drove back in it to the Essex.
On the way Haze told him about the Church Without
Christ; he explained its principles and said there was no
such thing as a bastard in it. The man didn't comment.
When they got out at the Essex, he put a can of gas in the
tank and Haze got in and tried to start it but nothing happened. The man opened up the hood and studied the inside for a while. He was a one-armed man with two sandy-
colored teeth and eyes that were slate-blue and thoughtful.
He had not spoken more than two words yet. He looked
for a long time under the hood while Haze stood by, but
he didn't touch anything. After a while he shut it and blew
his nose.

"What's wrong in there?" Haze asked in an agitated
voice. "It's a good car, ain't it?"

The man didn't answer him. He sat down on the ground
and eased under the Essex. He wore hightop shoes and

gray socks. He stayed under the car a long time. Haze got down on his hands and knees and looked under to see what he was doing but he wasn't doing anything. He was just lying there, looking up, as if he were contemplating; his good arm was folded on his chest. After a while, he eased himself out and wiped his face and neck with a piece of flannel rag he had in his pocket.

"Listenhere," Haze said, "that's a good car. You just give me a push, that's all. That car'll get me anywhere I want to go."

The man didn't say anything but he got back in the truck and Haze and Sabbath Hawks got in the Essex and he pushed them. After a few hundred yards the Essex began to belch and gasp and jiggle. Haze stuck his head out the window and motioned for the truck to come alongside. "Ha!" he said. "I told you, didn't I? This car'll get me anywhere I want to go. It may stop here and there but it won't stop permanent. What do I owe you?"

"Nothing," the man said, "not a thing."

"But the gas," Haze said, "how much for the gas?"

"Nothing," the man said with the same level look. "Not a thing."

"All right, I thank you," Haze said and drove on. "I don't need no favors from him," he said.

"It's a grand auto," Sabbath Hawks said. "It goes as smooth as honey."

"It ain't been built by a bunch of foreigners or niggers

or one-arm men," Haze said. "It was built by people with their eyes open that knew where they were at."

When they came to the end of the dirt road and were facing the paved one, the pick-up truck pulled alongside again and while the two cars paused side by side, Haze and the slate-eyed man looked at each other out of their two windows. "I told you this car would get me anywhere I wanted to go," Haze said sourly.

"Some things," the man said, " 'll get some folks somewheres," and he turned the truck up the highway.

Haze drove on. The blinding white cloud had turned into a bird with long thin wings and was disappearing in the opposite direction.

CHAPTER 8

Enoch Emery knew now that his life would never be the same again, because the thing that was going to happen to him had started to happen. He had always known that something was going to happen but he hadn't known what. If he had been much given to thought, he might have thought that now was the time for him to justify his daddy's blood, but he didn't think in broad sweeps like that, he thought what he would do next. Sometimes he didn't think, he only wondered; then before long he would find himself doing this or that, like a bird finds itself building a nest when it hasn't actually been planning to.

What was going to happen to him had started to happen when he showed what was in the glass case to Haze Motes. That was a mystery beyond his understanding, but he knew that what was going to be expected of him was something awful. His blood was more sensitive than any other part of him; it wrote doom all through him, except possibly in his brain, and the result was that his tongue, which edged out every few minutes to test his fever blister, knew more than he did.

The first thing that he found himself doing that was not normal was saving his pay. He was saving all of it, except what his landlady came to collect every week and what he had to use to buy something to eat with. Then to his surprise, he found he wasn't eating very much and he was saving that money too. He had a fondness for Supermarkets; it was his custom to spend an hour or so in one every afternoon after he left the city park, browsing around among the canned goods and reading the cereal stories. Lately he had been compelled to pick up a few things here and there that would not be bulky in his pockets, and he wondered if this could be the reason he was saving so much money on food. It could have been, but he had the suspicion that saving the money was connected with some larger thing. He had always been given to stealing but he had never saved before.

At the same time, he began cleaning up his room. It was a little green room, or it had once been green, in the attic of an elderly rooming house. There was a mummified look and feel to this residence, but Enoch had never thought before of brightening the part (corresponding to the head) that he lived in. Then he simply found himself doing it.

First, he removed the rug from the floor and hung it out the window. This was a mistake because when he went to pull it back in, there were only a few long strings left with a carpet tack caught in one of them. He imagined that it must have been a very old rug and he decided to handle the rest of the furniture with more care. He washed the bed frame with soap and water and found that under the second layer of dirt, it was pure gold, and this affected him so strongly that he washed the chair. It was a low round chair that bulged around the legs so that it seemed to be in the act of squatting. The gold began to appear with the first touch of water but it disappeared with the second and with a little more, the chair sat down as if this were the end of long years of inner struggle. Enoch didn't know if it was for him or against him. He had a nasty impulse to kick it to pieces, but he let it stay there, exactly in the position it had sat down in, because for the time anyway, he was not a foolhardy boy who took chances on the meanings of things. For the time, he knew that what he didn't know was what mattered.

The only other piece of furniture in the room was a washstand. This was built in three parts and stood on bird legs six inches high. The legs had clawed feet that were each one gripped around a small cannon ball. The lowest part was a tabernacle-like cabinet which was meant to contain a slop-jar. Enoch didn't own a slop-jar but he had a certain reverence for the purpose of things and since he didn't have the right thing to put in it, he left it empty. Directly over this place for the treasure, there was a gray marble slab and coming up from behind it was a wooden trellis-work of hearts, scrolls and flowers, extending into a hunched eagle wing on either side, and containing in the middle, just at the level of Enoch's face when he stood in front of it, a small oval mirror. The wooden frame continued again over the mirror and ended in a crowned, horned headpiece, showing that the artist had not lost faith in his work.

As far as Enoch was concerned, this piece had always been the center of the room and the one that most connected him with what he didn't know. More than once after a big supper, he had dreamed of unlocking the cabinet and getting in it and then proceeding to certain rites and mysteries that he had a very vague idea about in the morning. In his cleaning up, his mind was on the washstand from the first, but as was usual with him, he began with the least important thing and worked around and in toward the center where the meaning was. So before he tackled the washstand, he took care of the pictures in the room.

These were three, one belonging to his landlady (who was almost totally blind but moved about by an acute sense of smell) and two of his own. Hers was a brown portrait of a moose standing in a small lake. The look of superiority on this animal's face was so insufferable to Enoch that, if he hadn't been afraid of him, he would have done something about it a long time ago. As it was, he couldn't do anything in his room but what the smug face was watching, not shocked because nothing better could be expected and not amused because nothing was funny. If he had looked all over for one, he couldn't have found a roommate that irritated him more. He kept up a constant stream of inner comment, uncomplimentary to the moose, though when he said anything aloud, he was more guarded. The moose was in a heavy brown frame with leaf designs on it and this added to his weight and his self-satisfied look. Enoch knew the time had come when something had to be done; he didn't know what was going to happen in his room, but when it happened, he didn't want to have the feeling that the moose was running it. The answer came to him fully prepared: he realized with a sudden intuition that taking the frame off him would be equal to taking the clothes off him (although he didn't have on any) and he was right because when he had done it, the animal looked so reduced that Enoch could only snicker and look at him out the corner of his eye.

After this success he turned his attention to the other two pictures. They were over calendars and had been sent him by the Hilltop Funeral Home and the American Rubber Tire Company. One showed a small boy in a pair of blue Doctor Denton sleepers, kneeling at his bed, saying, "And bless daddy," while the moon looked in at the window. This was Enoch's favorite painting and it hung directly over his bed. The other pictured a lady wearing a rubber tire and it hung directly across from the moose on the opposite wall. He left it where it was, pretty certain that the moose only pretended not to see it. Immediately after he finished with the pictures, he went out and bought chintz curtains, a bottle of gilt, and a paint brush with all the money he had saved.

This was a disappointment to him because he had hoped that the money would be for some new clothes for him, and here he saw it going into a set of drapes. He didn't know what the gilt was for until he got home with it; when he got home with it, he sat down in front of the slop-jar cabinet in the washstand, unlocked it, and painted the inside of it with the gilt. Then he realized that the cabinet was to be used FOR something.

Enoch never nagged his blood to tell him a thing until it was ready. He wasn't the kind of a boy who grabs at any possibility and runs off, proposing this or that preposterous thing. In a large matter like this, he was always willing to wait for a certainty, and he waited for this one, certain at least that he would know in a few days. Then for about a week his blood was in secret conference with itself every day, only stopping now and then to shout some order at him.

On the following Monday, he was certain when he woke up that today was the day he was going to know on. His blood was rushing around like a woman who cleans up the house after the company has come, and he was surly and rebellious. When he realized that today was the day, he decided not to get up. He didn't want to justify his daddy's blood, he didn't want to be always having to do something that something else wanted him to do, that he didn't know what it was and that was always dangerous.

Naturally, his blood was not going to put up with any attitude like this. He was at the zoo by nine-thirty, only a half-hour later than he was supposed to be. All morning his mind was not on the gate he was supposed to guard but was chasing around after his blood, like a boy with a mop and a bucket, beating something here and sloshing down something there, without a second's rest. As soon as the second-shift guard came, Enoch headed toward town.

Town was the last place he wanted to be because anything could happen there. All the time his mind had been chasing around it had been thinking how as soon as he got off duty he was going to sneak off home and go to bed.

By the time he got into the center of the business district he was exhausted and he had to lean against Walgreen's window and cool off. Sweat crept down his back and provoked him to itch so that in just a few minutes he appeared to be working his way across the glass by his muscles, against a background of alarm clocks, toilet waters, candies, sanitary pads, fountain pens, and pocket flashlights, displayed in all colors to twice his height. He appeared to be working his way to a rumbling noise which came from the center of a small alcove that formed the entrance to the drug store. Here was a yellow and blue, glass and steel machine, belching popcorn into a cauldron of butter and salt. Enoch approached, already with his purse out, sorting his money. His purse was a long gray leather pouch, tied at the top with a drawstring. It was one he had stolen from his daddy and he treasured it because it was the only thing he owned now that his daddy had touched (besides himself). He sorted out two nickels and handed them to a pasty boy in a white apron who was there to serve the machine. The boy felt around in its vitals and filled a white paper bag with the corn, not taking his eye off Enoch's purse the while. On any other day Enoch would have tried to make friends with him but today he was too preoccupied even to see him. He took the bag and began stuffing the pouch back where it had come from. The youth's eye followed to the very edge of the pocket. "That thang looks like a hawg bladder," he observed enviously.

"I got to go now," Enoch murmured and hurried into the drug store. Inside, he walked abstractedly to the back of the store, and then up to the front again by the other aisle as if he wanted any person who might be looking for him to see he was there. He paused in front of the soda fountain to see if he would sit down and have something to eat. The fountain counter was pink and green marble linoleum and behind it there was a red-headed waitress in a lime-colored uniform and a pink apron. She had green eyes set in pink and they resembled a picture behind her of a Lime-Cherry Surprise, a special that day for ten cents.

She confronted Enoch while he studied the information over her head. After a minute she laid her chest on the counter and surrounded it by her folded arms, to wait. Enoch couldn't decide which of several concoctions was the one for him to have until she ended it by moving one arm under the counter and bringing out a Lime-Cherry Surprise. "It's okay," she said, "I fixed it this morning after breakfast."

"Something's going to happen to me today," Enoch said.

"I told you it was okay," she said. "I fixed it today."

"I seen it this morning when I woke up," he said, with the look of a visionary.

"God," she said, and jerked it from under his face. She turned around and began slapping things together; in a second she slammed another—exactly like it, but fresh—in front of him.

"I got to go now," Enoch said, and hurried out. An eye caught at his pocket as he passed the popcorn machine but he didn't stop. I don't want to do it, he was saying to himself. Whatever it is, I don't want to do it. I'm going home. It'll be something I don't want to do. It'll be something I ain't got no business doing. And he thought of how he had had to spend all his money on drapes and gilt when he could have bought him a shirt and a phosphorescent tie. It'll be something against the law, he said. It's always something against the law. I ain't going to do it, he said, and stopped. He had stopped in front of a movie house where there was a large illustration of a monster stuffing a young woman into an incinerator.

I ain't going in no picture show like that, he said, giving it a nervous look. I'm going home. I ain't going to wait around in no picture show. I ain't got the money to buy a ticket, he said, taking out his purse again. I ain't even going to count thisyer change.

It ain't but forty-three cent here, he said, that ain't enough. A sign said the price of a ticket for adults was forty-five cents, balcony, thirty-five. I ain't going to sit in no balcony, he said, buying a thirty-five cent ticket.

I ain't going in, he said.

Two doors flew open and he found himself moving down a long red foyer and then up a darker tunnel and then up a higher, still darker tunnel. In a few minutes he was up in a high part of the maw, feeling around, like Jonah, for a seat. I ain't going to look at it, he said furiously. He didn't like any picture shows but colored musical ones.

The first picture was about a scientist named The Eye who performed operations by remote control. You would wake up in the morning and find a slit in your chest or head or stomach and something you couldn't do without would be gone. Enoch pulled his hat down very low and drew his knees up in front of his face; only his eyes looked at the screen. That picture lasted an hour.

The second picture was about life at Devil's Island Penitentiary. After a while, Enoch had to grip the two arms of his seat to keep himself from falling over the rail in front of him.

The third picture was called, "Lonnie Comes Home Again." It was about a baboon named Lonnie who rescued attractive children from a burning orphanage. Enoch kept hoping Lonnie would get burned up but he didn't appear to get even hot. In the end a nice-looking girl gave him a medal. It was more than Enoch could stand. He made a dive for the aisle, fell down the two higher tunnels, and raced out the red foyer and into the street. He collapsed as soon as the air hit him.

When he recovered himself, he was sitting against the wall of the picture show building and he was not thinking any more about escaping his duty. It was night and he had the feeling that the knowledge he couldn't avoid was almost on him. His resignation was perfect. He leaned against the wall for about twenty minutes and then he got up and began to walk down the street as if he were led by a silent melody or by one of those whistles that only dogs hear. At the end of two blocks he stopped, his attention directed across the street. There, facing him under a street light, was a high rat-colored car and up on the nose of it, a dark figure with a fierce white hat on. The figure's arms were working up and down and he had thin, gesticulating hands, almost as pale as the hat. "Hazel Motes!" Enoch breathed, and his heart began to slam from side to side like a wild bell clapper.

There were a few people standing on the sidewalk near the car. Enoch didn't know that Hazel Motes had started the Church Without Christ and was preaching it every night on the street; he hadn't seen him since that day at the park when he had showed him the shriveled man in the glass case.

"If you had been redeemed," Hazel Motes was shouting, "you would care about redemption but you don't. Look inside yourselves and see if you hadn't rather it wasn't if it was. There's no peace for the redeemed," he shouted, "and I preach peace, I preach the Church Without Christ, the church peaceful and satisfied!"

Two or three people who had stopped near the car started walking off the other way. "Leave!" Hazel Motes cried. "Go ahead and leave! The truth don't matter to you. Listen," he said, pointing his finger at the rest of them, "the truth don't matter to you. If Jesus had redeemed you, what difference would it make to you? You wouldn't do nothing about it. Your faces wouldn't move, neither this way nor that, and if it was three crosses there and Him hung on the middle one, that one wouldn't mean no more to you and me than the other two. Listen here. What you need is something to take the place of Jesus, something that would speak plain. The Church Without Christ don't have a Jesus but it needs one! It needs a new jesus! It needs one that's all man, without blood to waste, and it needs one that don't look like any other man so you'll look at him. Give me such a jesus, you people. Give me such a new jesus and you'll see how far the Church Without Christ can go!"

One of the people watching walked off so there were only two left. Enoch was standing in the middle of the street, paralyzed.

"Show me where this new jesus is," Hazel Motes cried, "and I'll set him up in the Church Without Christ and then you'll see the truth. Then you'll know once and for all that you haven't been redeemed. Give me this new jesus, somebody, so we'll all be saved by the sight of him!"

Enoch began shouting without a sound. He shouted that way for a full minute while Hazel Motes went on.

"Look at me!" Hazel Motes cried, with a tare in his throat, "and you look at a peaceful man! Peaceful because my blood has set me free. Take counsel from your blood and come into the Church Without Christ and maybe somebody will bring us a new jesus and we'll all be saved by the sight of him!"

An unintelligible sound spluttered out of Enoch. He tried to bellow, but his blood held him back. He whispered, "Listenhere, I got him! I mean I can get him! You know! Him! Him I shown you to. You seen him yourself!"

His blood reminded him that the last time he had seen Haze Motes was when Haze Motes had hit him over the head with a rock. And he didn't even know yet how he would steal it out of the glass case. The only thing he knew was that he had a place in his room prepared to keep it in until Haze was ready to take it. His blood suggested he just let it come as a surprise to Haze Motes. He began to back away. He backed across the street and over a piece of sidewalk and out into the other street and a taxi had to stop short to keep from hitting him. The driver put his head out the window and asked him how he got around so well when God had made him by putting two backs together instead of a back and a front.

Enoch was too preoccupied to think about it. "I got to go now," he murmured, and hurried off.

CHAPTER 9

Hawks kept his door bolted and whenever Haze knocked on it, which he did two or three times a day, the ex-evangelist sent his child out to him and bolted the door again behind her. It infuriated him to have Haze lurking in the house, thinking up some excuse to get in and look at his face; and he was often drunk and didn't want to be discovered that way.

Haze couldn't understand why the preacher didn't welcome him and act like a preacher should when he sees what he believes is a lost soul. He kept trying to get into the room again; the window he could have reached was kept locked and the shade pulled down. He wanted to see, if he could, *behind* the black glasses.

Every time he went to the door, the girl came out and the bolt shut inside; then he couldn't get rid of her. She followed him out to his car and climbed in and spoiled his rides or she followed him up to his room and sat. He abandoned the notion of seducing her and tried to protect himself. He hadn't been in the house a week before she appeared in his room one night after he had gone to bed. She was holding a candle burning in a jelly glass and wore, hanging onto her thin shoulders, a woman's nightgown that dragged on the floor behind her. Haze didn't wake up until she was almost up to his bed, and when he did, he sprang from under his cover into the middle of the room.

"What you want?" he said.

She didn't say anything and her grin widened in the candle light. He stood glowering at her for an instant and then he picked up the straight chair and raised it as if he were going to bring it down on her. She lingered only a fraction of a second. His door didn't bolt so he propped the chair under the knob before he went back to bed.

"Listen," she said when she got back to their room, "nothing works. He would have hit me with a chair."

"I'm leaving out of here in a couple of days," Hawks said, "you better make it work if you want to eat after I'm gone." He was drunk but he meant it.

Nothing was working the way Haze had expected it to. He had spent every evening preaching, but the membership of the Church Without Christ was still only one person: himself. He had wanted to have a large following quickly to impress the blind man with his powers, but no one had followed him. There had been a sort of follower but that had been a mistake. That had been a boy about sixteen years old who had wanted someone to go to a whorehouse with him because he had never been to one before. He knew where the place was but he didn't want to go without a person of experience, and when he heard Haze, he hung around until he stopped preaching and then asked him to go. But it was all a mistake because after they had gone and got out again and Haze had asked him to be a member of the Church Without Christ, or more than that, a disciple, an apostle, the boy said he was sorry but he couldn't be a member of that church because he was a Lapsed Catholic. He said that what they had just done was a mortal sin, and that should they die unrepentant of it they would suffer eternal punishment and never see God. Haze had not enjoyed the whorehouse anywhere near as much as the boy had and he had wasted half his evening. He shouted that there was no such thing as sin or judgment, but the boy only shook his head and asked him if he would like to go again the next night.

If Haze had believed in praying, he would have prayed for a disciple, but as it was all he could do was worry about it a lot. Then two nights after the boy, the disciple appeared.

That night he preached outside of four different picture shows and every time he looked up, he saw the same big face smiling at him. The man was plumpish, and he had curly blond hair that was cut with showy sideburns. He wore a black suit with a silver stripe in it and a wide-brimmed white hat pushed onto the back of his head, and he had on tight-fitting black pointed shoes and no socks. He looked like an ex-preacher turned cowboy, or an ex-cowboy turned mortician. He was not handsome but under his smile, there was an honest look that fitted into his face like a set of false teeth.

Every time Haze looked at him, the man winked.

At the last picture show he preached in front of, there were three people listening to him besides the man. "Do you people care anything about the truth?" he asked. "The only way to the truth is through blasphemy, but do you care? Are you going to pay any attention to what I've been saying or are you just going to walk off like everybody else?"

There were two men and a woman with a cat-faced baby sprawled over her shoulder. She had been looking at Haze as if he were in a booth at the fair. "Well, come on," she said, "he's finished. We got to be going." She turned away and the two men fell in behind her.

"Go ahead and go," Haze said, "but remember that the truth don't lurk around every street corner."

The man who had been following reached up quickly and pulled Haze's pantsleg and gave him a wink. "Come on back heah, you folks," he said. "I want to tell you all about *me*."

The woman turned around again and he smiled at her as if he had been struck all along with her good looks. She had a square red face and her hair was freshly set. "I wisht I had my gittarr here," the man said, " 'cause I just somehow can say sweet things to music bettern plain. And when you talk about Jesus you need a little music, don't you, friends?" He looked at the two men as if he were appealing to the good judgment that was impressed on their faces. They had on brown felt hats and black town suits, and they looked like older and younger brother. "Listen, friends," the disciple said confidentially, "two months ago before I met the Prophet here, you wouldn't know me for the same man. I didn't have a friend in the world. Do you know what it's like not to have a friend in the world?"

"It ain't no worsen havinum that would put a knife in your back when you wasn't looking," the older man said, barely parting his lips.

"Friend, you said a mouthful when you said that," the man said. "If we had time, I would have you repeat that just so ever'body could hear it like I did." The picture show was over and more people were coming up. "Friends," the man said, "I know you're all interested in the Prophet here," pointing to Haze on the nose of the car, "and if you'll just give me time I'm going to tell you what him and his idears've done for me. Don't crowd because I'm willing to stay here all night and tell you if it takes that long."

Haze stood where he was, motionless, with his head slightly forward, as if he weren't sure what he was hearing.

"Friends," the man said, "lemme innerduce myself. My

name is Onnie Jay Holy and I'm telling it to you so you can check up and see I don't tell you any lie. I'm a preacher and I don't mind who knows it but I wouldn't have you believe nothing you can't feel in your own hearts. You people coming up on the edge push right on up in here where you can hear good," he said. "I'm not selling a thing, I'm giving something away!" A considerable number of people had stopped.

"Friends," he said, "two months ago you wouldn't know me for the same man. I didn't have a friend in the world. Do you know what it's like not to have a friend in the world?"

A loud voice said, "It ain't no worsen havinum that would put . . ."

"Why, friends," Onnie Jay Holy said, "not to have a friend in the world is just about the most miserable and lonesome thing that can happen to a man or woman! And that's the way it was with me. I was ready to hang myself or to despair completely. Not even my own dear old mother loved me, and it wasn't because I wasn't sweet inside, it was because I never known how to make the natural sweetness inside me show. Every person that comes onto this earth," he said, stretching out his arms, "is born sweet and full of love. A little child loves ever'body, friends, and its nature is sweetness—until something happens. Something happens, friends, I don't need to tell people like you that can think for theirselves. As that little child gets bigger, its sweetness don't show so much, cares and troubles come to perplext it, and all its sweetness is driven inside it. Then it gets miserable and lonesome and sick, friends. It says, 'Where is all my sweetness gone? where are all the friends that loved me?' and all the time, that little beat-up rose of its sweetness is inside, not a petal dropped, and on the outside is just a mean lonesomeness. It may want to take its own life or yours or mine, or to despair completely, friends." He said it in a sad nasal voice but he was smiling all the time so that they could tell he had been through what he was talking about and come out on top. "That was the way it was with me, friends. I know what of I speak," he said, and folded his hands in front of him. "But all the time that I was ready to hang myself or to despair completely, I was sweet inside, like ever'body else, and I only needed something to bring it out. I only needed a little help, friends.

"Then I met this Prophet here," he said, pointing at Haze on the nose of the car. "That was two months ago, folks, that I heard how he was out to help me, how he was preaching the Church of Christ Without Christ, the church that was going to get a new jesus to help me bring my sweet nature into the open where ever'body could enjoy it. That was two months ago, friends, and now you wouldn't know me for the same man. I love ever'one of you people and I want you to listen to him and me and join our church, the Holy Church of Christ Without Christ, the new church with the new jesus, and then you'll all be helped like me!"

Haze leaned forward. "This man is not true," he said. "I never saw him before tonight. I wasn't preaching this church two months ago and the name of it ain't the Holy Church of Christ Without Christ!"

The man ignored this and so did the people. There were ten or twelve gathered around. "Friends," Onnie Jay Holy said, "I'm mighty glad you're seeing me now instead of two months ago because then I couldn't have testified to this new church and this Prophet here. If I had my gittarr with me I could say all this better but I'll just have to do the best I can by myself." He had a winning smile and it was evident that he didn't think he was any better than anybody else even though he was.

"Now I just want to give you folks a few reasons why you can trust this church," he said. "In the first place, friends, you can rely on it that it's nothing foreign connected with it. You don't have to believe nothing you don't understand and approve of. If you don't understand it, it ain't true, and that's all there is to it. No jokers in the deck, friends."

Haze leaned forward. "Blasphemy is the way to the truth," he said, "and there's no other way whether you understand it or not!"

"Now, friends," Onnie Jay said, "I want to tell you a second reason why you can absolutely trust this church—

it's based on the Bible. Yes sir! It's based on your own personal interpitation of the Bible, friends. You can sit at home and interpit your own Bible however you feel in your heart it ought to be interpited. That's right," he said, "just the way Jesus would have done it. Gee, I wisht I had my gittarr here," he complained.

"This man is a liar," Haze said. "I never saw him before tonight. I never . . ."

"That ought to be enough reasons, friends," Onnie Jay Holy said, "but I'm going to tell you one more, just to show I can. This church is up-to-date! When you're in this church you can know that there's nothing or nobody ahead of you, nobody knows nothing you don't know, all the cards are on the table, friends, and that's a fack!"

Haze's face under the white hat began to take on a look of fierceness. Just as he was about to open his mouth again, Onnie Jay Holy pointed in astonishment to the baby in the blue bonnet who was sprawled limp over the woman's shoulder. "Why yonder is a little babe," he said, "a little bundle of helpless sweetness. Why, I know you people aren't going to let that little thing grow up and have all his sweetness pushed inside him when it could be on the outside to win friends and make him loved. That's why I want ever' one of you people to join the Holy Church of Christ Without Christ. It'll cost you each a dollar but what is a dollar? A few dimes! Not too much to pay to unlock that little rose of sweetness inside you!"

"Listen!" Haze shouted. "It don't cost you any money to know the truth! You can't know it for money!"

"You hear what the Prophet says, friends," Onnie Jay Holy said, "a dollar is not too much to pay. No amount of money is too much to learn the truth! Now I want each of you people that are going to take advantage of this church to sign on this little pad I have in my pocket here and give me your dollar personally and let me shake your hand!"

Haze slid down from the nose of his car and got in it and slammed his foot on the starter.

"Hey wait! Wait!" Onnie Jay Holy shouted, "I ain't got any of these friends' names yet!"

The Essex had a tendency to develop a tic by nightfall. It would go forward about six inches and then back about four; it did that now a succession of times rapidly; otherwise Haze would have shot off in it and been gone. He had to grip the steering wheel with both hands to keep from being thrown either out the windshield or into the back. It stopped this after a few seconds and slid about twenty feet and then began it again.

Onnie Jay Holy's face showed a great strain; he put his hand to the side of it as if the only way he could keep his smile on was to hold it. "I got to go now, friends," he said quickly, "but I'll be at this same spot tomorrow night, I got to go catch the Prophet now," and he ran off just as the Essex began to slide again. He wouldn't have caught it, except that it stopped before it had gone ten feet farther.

He jumped on the running board and got the door open and plumped in, panting, beside Haze. "Friend," he said, "we just lost ten dollars. What you in such a hurry for?" His face showed that he was in some kind of genuine pain even though he looked at Haze with a smile that revealed all his upper teeth and the tops of his lowers.

Haze turned his head and looked at him long enough to see the smile before it was thrown forward at the windshield. After that the Essex began running smoothly. Onnie Jay took out a lavender handkerchief and held it in front of his mouth for some time. When he removed it, the smile was back on his face. "Friend," he said, "you and me have to get together on this thing. I said when I first heard you open your mouth, 'Why, yonder is a great man with great idears.' "

Haze didn't turn his head.

Onnie Jay took in a long breath. "Why, do you know who you put me in mind of when I first saw you?" he asked. After a minute of waiting, he said in a soft voice, "Jesus Christ and Abraham Lincoln, friend."

Haze's face was suddenly swamped with outrage. All the expression on it was obliterated. "You ain't true," he said in a barely audible voice.

"Friend, how can you say that?" Onnie Jay said. "Why I was on the radio for three years with a program that give real religious experiences to the whole family. Didn't you ever listen to it—called, Soulsease, a quarter hour of Mood, Melody, and Mentality? I'm a real preacher, friend."

Haze stopped the Essex. "You get out," he said.

"Why friend!" Onnie Jay said. "You ought not to say such a thing! That's the absolute truth that I'm a preacher and a radio star."

"Get out," Haze said, reaching across and opening the door for him.

"I never thought you would treat a friend thisaway," Onnie Jay said. "All I wanted to ast you about was this new jesus."

"Get out," Haze said, and began to push him toward the door. He pushed him to the edge of the seat and gave him a shove and Onnie Jay fell out the door and into the road.

"I never thought a friend would treat me thisaway," he complained. Haze kicked his leg off the running board and shut the door again. He put his foot on the starter but nothing happened except a noise somewhere underneath him that sounded like a person gargling without water. Onnie Jay got up off the pavement and stood at the window. "If you would just tell me where this new jesus is you was mentioning," he began.

Haze put his foot on the starter a succession of times but nothing happened.

"Pull out the choke," Onnie Jay advised, getting up on the running board.

"There's no choke on it," Haze snarled.

"Maybe it's flooded," Onnie Jay said. "While we're waiting, you and me can talk about the Holy Church of Christ Without Christ."

"My church is the Church Without Christ," Haze said. "I've seen all of you I want to."

"It don't make any difference how many Christs you add to the name if you don't add none to the meaning, friend," Onnie Jay said in a hurt tone. "You ought to listen to me because I'm not just an amateur. I'm an artist-type. If you want to get anywheres in religion, you got to keep it sweet. You got good idears but what you need is an artist-type to work with you."

Haze rammed his foot on the gas and then on the starter and then on the starter and then on the gas. Nothing happened. The street was practically deserted. "Me and you could get behind it and push it over to the curb," Onnie Jay suggested.

"I ain't asked for your help," Haze said.

"You know, friend, I certainly would like to see this new jesus," Onnie Jay said. "I never heard a idear before that had more in it than that one. All it would need is a little promotion."

Haze tried to start the car by forcing his weight forward on the steering wheel, but that didn't work. He got out and got behind it and began to push it over to the curb. Onnie Jay got behind with him and added his weight. "I kind of have had that idear about a new jesus myself," he remarked. "I seen how a new one would be more up-to-date.

"Where you keeping him, friend?" he asked. "Is he somebody you see ever' day? I certainly would like to meet him and hear some of his idears."

They pushed the car into a parking space. There was no way to lock it and Haze was afraid that if he left it out all night so far away from where he lived someone would be able to steal it. There was nothing for him to do but sleep in it. He got in the back and began to pull down the fringed shades. Onnie Jay had his head in the front, however. "You needn't to be afraid that if I seen this new jesus I would cut you out of anything," he said. "Why friend, it would just mean a lot to me for the good of my spirit."

Haze moved the two-by-four off the seat frame to make more room to fix up his pallet. He kept a pillow and an army blanket back there and he had a sterno stove and a coffee pot up on the shelf under the back oval window. "Friend, I would even be glad to pay you a little something to see him," Onnie Jay suggested.

"Listen here," Haze said, "you get away from here. I've seen all of you I want to. There's no such thing as any new jesus. That ain't anything but a way to say something."

The smile more or less slithered off Onnie Jay's face. "What you mean by that?" he asked.

"That there's no such thing or person," Haze said. "It

wasn't nothing but a way to say a thing." He put his hand on the door handle and began to close it in spite of Onnie Jay's head. "No such thing exists!" he shouted.

"That's the trouble with you innerleckchuls," Onnie Jay muttered, "you don't never have nothing to show for what you're saying."

"Get your head out my car door, Holy," Haze said.

"My name is Hoover Shoats," the man with his head in the door growled. "I known when I first seen you that you wasn't nothing but a crackpot."

Haze opened the door enough to be able to slam it. Hoover Shoats got his head out the way but not his thumb. A howl arose that would have rended almost any heart. Haze opened the door and released the thumb and then slammed the door again. He pulled down the front shades and lay down in the back of the car on the army blanket. Outside he could hear Hoover Shoats jumping around on the pavement and howling. When the howls died down, Haze heard a few steps up to the car and then an impassioned, breathless voice say through the tin, "You watch out, friend. I'm going to run you out of business. I can get my own new jesus and I can get Prophets for peanuts, you hear? Do you hear me, friend?" the hoarse voice said.

Haze didn't answer.

"Yeah and I'll be out there doing my own preaching tomorrow night. What you need is a little competition," the voice said. "Do you hear me, friend?"

Haze got up and leaned over the front seat and banged his hand down on the horn of the Essex. It made a sound like a goat's laugh cut off with a buzz saw. Hoover Shoats jumped back as if a charge of electricity had gone through him. "All right, friend," he said, standing about fifteen feet away, trembling, "you just wait, you ain't heard the last of me yet," and he turned and went off down the quiet street.

Haze stayed in his car about an hour and had a bad experience in it: he dreamed he was not dead but only buried. He was not waiting on the Judgment because there was no Judgment, he was waiting on nothing. Various eyes looked through the back oval window at his situation, some with considerable reverence, like the boy from the zoo, and some only to see what they could see. There were three women with paper sacks who looked at him critically as if he were something—a piece of fish—they might buy, but they passed on after a minute. A man in a canvas hat looked in and put his thumb to his nose and wiggled his fingers. Then a woman with two little boys on either side of her stopped and looked in, grinning. After a second, she pushed the boys out of view and indicated that she would climb in and keep him company for a while, but she couldn't get through the glass and finally she went off. All this time Haze was bent on getting out but since there was no use to try, he didn't make any move one way or the other. He kept expecting Hawks to appear at the oval window with a wrench, but the blind man didn't come.

Finally he shook off the dream and woke up. He thought it should be morning but it was only midnight. He pulled himself over into the front of the car and eased his foot on the starter and the Essex rolled off quietly as if nothing were the matter with it. He drove back to the house and let himself in but instead of going upstairs to his room, he stood in the hall, looking at the blind man's door. He went over to it and put his ear to the keyhole and heard the sound of snoring; he turned the knob gently but the door didn't move.

For the first time, the idea of picking the lock occurred to him. He felt in his pockets for an instrument and came on a small piece of wire that he sometimes used for a tooth-pick. There was only a dim light in the hall but it was enough for him to work by and he knelt down at the key-hole and inserted the wire into it carefully, trying not to make a noise.

After a while when he had tried the wire five or six different ways, there was a slight click in the lock. He stood up, trembling, and opened the door. His breath came short and his heart was palpitating as if he had run all the way here from a great distance. He stood just inside the room until his eyes got accustomed to the darkness and then he moved slowly over to the iron bed and stood there. Hawks was lying across it. His head was hanging over the edge. Haze squatted down by him and struck a match close to his face and he opened his eyes. The two sets of eyes looked at each other as long as the match lasted; Haze's expression seemed to open onto a deeper blankness and reflect something and then close again.

"Now you can get out," Hawks said in a short thick voice, "now you can leave me alone," and he made a jab at the face over him without touching it. It moved back, expressionless under the white hat, and was gone in a second.

CHAPTER 10

The next night, Haze parked the Essex in front of the Odeon Theater and climbed up on it and began to preach. "Let me tell you what I and this church stand for!" he called from the nose of the car. "Stop one minute to listen to the truth because you may never hear it again." He stood there with his neck thrust forward, moving one arm upward in a vague arc. Two women and a boy stopped.

"I preach there are all kinds of truth, your truth and somebody else's, but behind all of them, there's only one truth and that is that there's no truth," he called. "No truth behind all truths is what I and this church preach! Where you come from is gone, where you thought you were going to never was there, and where you are is no good unless you can get away from it. Where is there a place for you to be? No place.

"Nothing outside you can give you any place," he said. "You needn't to look at the sky because it's not going to open up and show no place behind it. You needn't to search for any hole in the ground to look through into somewhere else. You can't go neither forwards nor backwards into your daddy's time nor your children's if you have them. In yourself right now is all the place you've got. If there was any Fall, look there, if there was any Redemption, look there, and if you expect any Judgment, look there, because they all three will have to be in your time and your body and where in your time and your body can they be?

"Where in your time and your body has Jesus redeemed you?" he cried. "Show me where because I don't see the place. If there was a place where Jesus had redeemed you that would be the place for you to be, but which of you can find it?"

Another trickle of people came out of the Odeon and two stopped to look at him. "Who is that that says it's your conscience?" he cried, looking around with a constricted face as if he could smell the particular person who thought that. "Your conscience is a trick," he said, "it don't exist though you may think it does, and if you think it does, you had best get it out in the open and hunt it down and kill it, because it's no more than your face in the mirror is or your shadow behind you."

He was preaching with such concentration that he didn't notice a high rat-colored car that had been driven around the block three times already, while the two men in it hunted a place to park. He didn't see it when it pulled in two cars over from him in a space that another car had just pulled out of, and he didn't see Hoover Shoats and a man in a glare-blue suit and white hat get out of it, but after a few seconds, his head turned that way and he saw the man in the glare-blue suit and white hat up on the nose of it. He was so struck with how gaunt and thin he looked in the illusion that he stopped preaching. He had never pictured himself that way before. The man he saw was hollow-chested and carried his neck thrust forward and his arms down by his side; he stood there as if he were waiting for some signal he was afraid he might not catch.

Hoover Shoats was walking about on the sidewalk, strik-ing a few chords on his guitar. "Friends," he called, "I want to innerduce you to the True Prophet here and I want you all to listen to his words because I think they're going to make you happy like they've made me!" If Haze had noticed Hoover he might have been impressed by how happy he looked, but his attention was fixed on the man on the nose of the car. He slid down from his own car and moved up closer, never taking his eyes from the bleak figure. Hoover Shoats raised his hand with two fingers pointed and the man suddenly cried out in a high nasal singsong voice. "The unredeemed are redeeming theirselves and the new jesus is at hand! Watch for this miracle! Help your-self to salvation in the Holy Church of Christ Without Christ!" He called it over again in exactly the same tone of voice, but faster. Then he began to cough. He had a loud consumptive cough that started somewhere deep in him and finished with a long wheeze. He expectorated a white fluid at the end of it.

Haze was standing next to a fat woman who after a minute turned her head and stared at him and then turned it again and stared at the True Prophet. Finally she touched his elbow with hers and grinned at him. "Him and you twins?" she asked.

"If you don't hunt it down and kill it, it'll hunt you down and kill you," Haze answered.

"Huh? Who?" she said.

He turned away and she stared at him as he got back in his car and drove off. Then she touched the elbow of a man on the other side of her. "He's nuts," she said. "I never seen no twins that hunted each other down."

When he got back to his room, Sabbath Hawks was in his bed. She was pushed over into one corner of it, sitting with one arm drawn around her knees and one hand holding onto the sheet as if she meant to hang on by it. Her face was sullen and apprehensive. Haze sat down on the bed but he barely glanced at her. "I don't care if you hit me with the table," she said. "I'm not going. There's no place for me to go. He's run off on me and it was you run him off. I was watching last night and I seen you come in and hold that match to his face. I thought anybody would have seen what he was before that without having to strike no match. He's just a crook. He ain't even a big crook, just a little one, and when he gets tired of that, he begs on the street."

Haze leaned down and began untying his shoes. They were old army shoes that he had painted black to get the government off. He untied them and eased his feet out and sat there looking down, while she watched him cautiously.

"Are you going to hit me or not?" she asked. "If you are, go ahead and do it right now because I'm not going. I ain't got any place to go." He didn't look as if he were going to hit anything; he looked as if he were going to sit there until he died. "Listen," she said, with a quick change of tone, "from the minute I set eyes on you I said to myself, that's what I got to have, just give me some of him! I said look at those pee-can eyes and go crazy, girl! That innocent look don't hide a thing, he's just pure filthy right down to the guts, like me. The only difference is I like being that way and he don't. Yes sir!" she said. "I like being that way, and I can teach you how to like it. Don't you want to learn how to like it?"

He turned his head slightly and just over his shoulder he saw a pinched homely little face with bright green eyes and a grin. "Yeah," he said with no change in his stony expression, "I want to." He stood up and took off his coat and his trousers and his drawers and put them on the straight chair. Then he turned off the light and sat down on the cot again and pulled off his socks. His feet were big and white and damp to the floor and he sat there, looking at the two white shapes they made.

"Come on! Make haste," she said, knocking his back with her knee.

He unbuttoned his shirt and took it off and wiped his face with it and dropped it on the floor. Then he slid his legs under the cover by her and sat there as if he were waiting to remember one more thing.

She was breathing very quickly. "Take off your hat, king of the beasts," she said gruffly and her hand came up behind his head and snatched the hat off and sent it flying across the room in the dark.

CHAPTER 11

The next morning toward noon a person in a long black raincoat, with a lightish hat pulled down low on his face and the brim of it turned down to meet the turned-up collar of the raincoat, was moving rapidly along certain back streets, close to the walls of the buildings. He was carrying something about the size of a baby, wrapped up in newspapers, and he carried a dark umbrella too, as the sky was an unpredictable surly gray like the back of an old goat. He had on a pair of dark glasses and a black beard which a keen observer would have said was not a natural growth but was pinned onto his hat on either side with safety pins. As he walked along, the umbrella kept slipping from under his arm and getting tangled in his feet, as if it meant to keep him from going anywhere.

He had not gone half a block before large putty-colored drops began to splatter on the pavement and there was an ugly growl in the sky behind him. He began to run, clutching the bundle in one arm and the umbrella in the other.

In a second, the storm overtook him and he ducked between two show-windows into the blue and white tiled entrance of a drug store. He lowered his dark glasses a little. The pale eyes that looked over the rims belonged to Enoch Emery. Enoch was on his way to Hazel Motes's room.

He had never been to Hazel Motes's place before but the instinct that was guiding him was very sure of itself. What was in the bundle was what he had shown Hazel at the museum. He had stolen it the day before.

He had darkened his face and hands with brown shoe polish so that if he were seen in the act, he would be taken for a colored person; then he had sneaked into the museum while the guard was asleep and had broken the glass case with a wrench he'd borrowed from his landlady; then, shaking and sweating, he had lifted the shriveled man out and thrust him in a paper sack, and had crept out again past the guard, who was still asleep. He realized as soon as he got out of the museum that since no one had seen him to think he was a colored boy, he would be suspected immediately and would have to disguise himself. That was why he had on the black beard and dark glasses.

When he'd got back to his room, he had taken the new jesus out of the sack and, hardly daring to look at him, had laid him in the gilted cabinet; then he had sat down on the edge of his bed to wait. He was waiting for something to happen, he didn't know what. He knew something was going to happen and his entire system was waiting on it. He thought it was going to be one of the supreme moments in his life but apart from that, he didn't have the vaguest notion what it might be. He pictured himself, after it was over, as an entirely new man, with an even better personality than he had now. He sat there for about fifteen minutes and nothing happened.

He sat there for about five more.

Then he realized that he had to make the first move. He got up and tiptoed to the cabinet and squatted down at the door of it; in a second he opened it a crack and looked in. After a while, very slowly, he broadened the crack and inserted his head into the tabernacle.

Some time passed.

From directly behind him, only the soles of his shoes and the seat of his trousers were visible. The room was absolutely silent; there was no sound even from the street; the Universe might have been shut off; not a flea jumped. Then without any warning, a loud liquid noise burst from the cabinet and there was the thump of bone cracked once against a piece of wood. Enoch staggered backward, clutching his head and his face. He sat on the floor for a few minutes with a shocked expression on his whole figure. At the first instant, he had thought it was the shriveled man who had sneezed, but after a second, he perceived the condition of his own nose. He wiped it off with his sleeve and then he sat there on the floor for some time longer. His expression had showed that a deep unpleasant knowledge was breaking on him slowly. After a while he had kicked the ark door shut in the new jesus' face, and then he had got up and begun to eat a candy bar very rapidly. He had eaten it as if he had something against it.

The next morning he had not got up until ten o'clock—it was his day off—and he had not set out until nearly noon to look for Hazel Motes. He remembered the address Sabbath Hawks had given him and that was where his instinct was leading him. He was very sullen and disgruntled at having to spend his day off in such a way as this, and in bad weather, but he wanted to get rid of the new jesus so that if the police had to catch anybody for the robbery, they could catch Hazel Motes instead of him. He couldn't understand at all why he had let himself risk his skin for a dead shriveled-up part-nigger dwarf that had never done anything but get himself embalmed and then lain stinking in a museum the rest of his life. It was far beyond his understanding. He was very sullen. So far as he was now concerned, one jesus was as bad as another.

He had borrowed his landlady's umbrella and he discovered as he stood in the entrance of the drug store, trying to open it, that it was at least as old as she was. When he finally got it hoisted, he pushed his dark glasses back on his eyes and re-entered the downpour.

The umbrella was one his landlady had stopped using fifteen years before (which was the only reason she had lent it to him) and as soon as the rain touched the top of it, it came down with a shriek and stabbed him in the back of the neck. He ran a few feet with it over his head and then backed into another store entrance and removed it. Then to get it up again, he had to place the tip of it on the ground and ram it open with his foot. He ran out again, holding his hand up near the spokes to keep them open and this allowed the handle, which was carved to represent the head of a fox terrier, to jab him every few seconds in the stomach. He proceeded for another quarter of a block this way before the back half of the silk stood up off the spokes and allowed the storm to sweep down his collar. Then he ducked under the marquee of a movie house. It was Saturday and there were a lot of children standing more or less in a line in front of the ticket box.

Enoch was not very fond of children but children always seemed to like to look at him. The line turned and twenty or thirty eyes began to observe him with a steady interest. The umbrella had assumed an ugly position, half up and half down, and the half that was up was about to come down and spill more water under his collar. When this happened the children laughed and jumped up and down. Enoch glared at them and turned his back and lowered his dark glasses. He found himself facing a life-size four-color picture of a gorilla. Over the gorilla's head, written in red letters was, "GONGA! Giant Jungle Monarch and a Great Star! HERE IN PERSON! ! !" At the level of the gorilla's knee, there was more that said, "Gonga will appear in person in front of this theater at 12 A.M. *TODAY!* A free pass to the first ten brave enough to step up and shake his hand!"

Enoch was usually thinking of something else at the moment that Fate began drawing back her leg to kick him. When he was four years old, his father had brought him home a tin box from the penitentiary. It was orange and had a picture of some peanut brittle on the outside of it and green letters that said, A NUTTY SURPRISE! When Enoch had opened it, a coiled piece of steel had sprung out at him and broken off the ends of his two front teeth. His life was full of so many happenings like that that it would seem he should have been more sensitive to his times of danger. He stood there and read the poster twice through carefully. To his mind, an opportunity to insult a successful ape came from the hand of Providence. He suddenly regained all his reverence for the new jesus. He saw that he was going to be rewarded after all and have the supreme moment he had expected.

He turned around and asked the nearest child what time it was. The child said it was twelve-ten and that Gonga was already ten minutes late. Another child said that maybe the rain had delayed him. Another said, no not the rain, his director was taking a plane from Hollywood. Enoch gritted his teeth. The first child said that if he wanted to shake the star's hand, he would have to get in line like the rest of them and wait his turn. Enoch got in line. A child asked him how old he was. Another observed that he had funny-looking teeth. He ignored all this as best he could and began to straighten out the umbrella.

In a few minutes a black truck turned around the corner and came slowly up the street in the heavy rain. Enoch pushed the umbrella under his arm and began to squint through his dark glasses. As the truck approached, a phonograph inside it began to play "Tarara Boom Di Aye," but the music was almost drowned out by the rain. There was a large illustration of a blonde on the outside of the truck, advertising some picture other than the gorilla's.

The children held their line carefully as the truck stopped in front of the movie house. The back door of it was constructed like a paddy wagon, with a grate, but the ape was not at it. Two men in raincoats got out of the cab part, cursing, and ran around to the back and opened the door. One of them stuck his head in and said, "Okay, make it snappy, willya?" The other jerked his thumb at the children and said, "Get back willya, willya get back?"

A voice on the record inside the truck said, "Here's Gonga, folks, Roaring Gonga and a Great Star! Give Gonga a big hand, folks!" The voice was barely a mumble in the rain.

The man who was waiting by the door of the truck stuck his head in again. "Okay willya get out?" he said.

There was a faint thump somewhere inside the van. After a second a dark furry arm emerged just enough for the rain to touch it and then drew back inside.

"Goddam," the man who was under the marquee said; he took off his raincoat and threw it to the man by the door, who threw it into the wagon. After two or three minutes more, the gorilla appeared at the door, with the raincoat buttoned up to his chin and the collar turned up. There was an iron chain hanging from around his neck; the man grabbed it and pulled him down and the two of them bounded under the marquee together. A motherly-looking woman was in the glass ticket box, getting the passes ready for the first ten children brave enough to step up and shake hands.

The gorilla ignored the children entirely and followed the man over to the other side of the entrance where there was a small platform raised about a foot off the ground. He stepped up on it and turned facing the children and began to growl. His growls were not so much loud as poisonous; they appeared to issue from a black heart. Enoch was terrified and if he had not been surrounded by the children, he would have run away.

"Who'll step up first?" the man said. "Come on come on, who'll step up first? A free pass to the first kid stepping up."

There was no movement from the group of children. The man glared at them. "What's the matter with you kids?" he barked. "You yellow? He won't hurt you as long as I got him by this chain." He tightened his grip on the chain and jangled it at them to show he was holding it securely.

After a minute a little girl separated herself from the group. She had long wood-shaving curls and a fierce triangular face. She moved up to within four feet of the star.

"Okay okay," the man said, rattling the chain, "make it snappy."

The ape reached out and gave her hand a quick shake. By this time there was another little girl ready and then two boys. The line re-formed and began to move up.

The gorilla kept his hand extended and turned his head away with a bored look at the rain. Enoch had got over his fear and was trying frantically to think of an obscene remark that would be suitable to insult him with. Usually he didn't have any trouble with this kind of composition but nothing came to him now. His brain, both parts, was completely empty. He couldn't think even of the insulting phrases he used every day.

There were only two children in front of him by now. The first one shook hands and stepped aside. Enoch's heart was beating violently. The child in front of him finished and stepped aside and left him facing the ape, who took his hand with an automatic motion.

It was the first hand that had been extended to Enoch since he had come to the city. It was warm and soft.

For a second he only stood there, clasping it. Then he began to stammer. "My name is Enoch Emery," he mumbled. "I attended the Rodemill Boys' Bible Academy. I work at the city zoo. I seen two of your pictures. I'm only eighteen year old but I already work for the city. My daddy made me com . . ." and his voice cracked.

The star leaned slightly forward and a change came in his eyes: an ugly pair of human ones moved closer and squinted at Enoch from behind the celluloid pair. "You go to hell," a surly voice inside the ape-suit said, low but distinctly, and the hand was jerked away.

Enoch's humiliation was so sharp and painful that he turned around three times before he realized which direction he wanted to go in. Then he ran off into the rain as fast as he could.

By the time he reached Sabbath Hawks's house, he was soaked through and so was his bundle. He held it in a fierce grip but all he wanted was to get rid of it and never see it again. Haze's landlady was out on the porch, looking distrustfully into the storm. He found out from her where Haze's room was and went up to it. The door was ajar and he stuck his head in the crack. Haze was lying on his cot, with a washrag over his eyes; the exposed part of his face was ashen and set in a grimace, as if he were in some permanent pain. Sabbath Hawks was sitting at the table by the window, studying herself in a pocket mirror. Enoch scratched on the wall and she looked up. She put the mirror

down and tiptoed out into the hall and shut the door behind her.

"My man is sick today and sleeping," she said, "because
he didn't sleep none last night. What you want?"

"This is for him, it ain't for you," Enoch said, handing
her the wet bundle. "A friend of his give it to me to give
to him. I don't know what's in it."

"I'll take care of it," she said. "You needn't to worry
none."

Enoch had an urgent need to insult somebody immediately; it was the only thing that could give his feelings
even a temporary relief. "I never known he would have
nothing to do with you," he remarked, giving her one of
his special looks.

"He couldn't leave off following me," she said. "Sometimes it's thataway with them. You don't know what's in
this package?"

"Lay-overs to catch meddlers," he said. "You just give
it to him and he'll know what it is and you can tell him
I'm glad to get shut of it." He started down the stairs and
halfway he turned and gave her another special look. "I see
why he has to put theter washrag over his eyes," he said.

"You keep your beeswax in your ears," she said. "Nobody asked you." When she heard the front door slam behind him, she turned the bundle over and began to examine it. There was no telling from the outside what was
in it; it was too hard to be clothes and too soft to be a

machine. She tore a hole in the paper at one end and saw what looked like five dried peas in a row but the hall was too dark for her to see clearly what they were. She decided to take the package to the bathroom, where there was a good light, and open it up before she gave it to Haze. If he was so sick as he said he was, he wouldn't want to be bothered with any bundle.

Early that morning he had claimed to have a terrible pain in his chest. He had begun to cough during the night— a hard hollow cough that sounded as if he were making it up as he went along. She was certain he was only trying to drive her off by letting her think he had a catching disease.

He's not really sick, she said to herself going down the hall, he just ain't used to me yet. She went in and sat down on the edge of a large green claw-footed tub and ripped the string off the package. "But he'll get used to me," she muttered. She pulled off the wet paper and let it fall on the floor; then she sat with a stunned look, staring at what was in her lap.

Two days out of the glass case had not improved the new jesus' condition. One side of his face had been partly mashed in and on the other side, his eyelid had split and a pale dust was seeping out of it. For a while her face had an empty look, as if she didn't know what she thought about him or didn't think anything. She might have sat there for ten minutes, without a thought, held by whatever it was that was familiar about him. She had never known

anyone who looked like him before, but there was something in him of everyone she had ever known, as if they
had all been rolled into one person and killed and shrunk
and dried.

She held him up and began to examine him and after a
minute her hands grew accustomed to the feel of his skin.
Some of his hair had come undone and she brushed it back
where it belonged, holding him in the crook of her arm
and looking down into his squinched face. His mouth had
been knocked a little to one side so that there was just a
trace of a grin covering his terrified look. She began to
rock him a little in her arm and a slight reflection of the
same grin appeared on her own face. "Well I declare," she
murmured, "you're right cute, ain't you?"

His head fitted exactly into the hollow of her shoulder.
"Who's your momma and daddy?" she asked.

An answer came into her mind at once and she let out a
short little bark and sat grinning, with a pleased expression
in her eyes. "Well, let's go give him a jolt," she said after
a while.

Haze had already been jolted awake when the front door
slammed behind Enoch Emery. He had sat up and seeing
she was not in the room, he had jumped up and begun to
put on his clothes. He had one thought in mind and it
had come to him, like his decision to buy a car, out of his
sleep and without any indication of it beforehand: he was
going to move immediately to some other city and preach

185

the Church Without Christ where they had never heard of it. He would get another room there and another woman and make a new start with nothing on his mind. The entire possibility of this came from the advantage of having a car—of having something that moved fast, in privacy, to the place you wanted to be. He looked out the window at the Essex. It sat high and square in the pouring rain. He didn't notice the rain, only the car; if asked he would not have been able to say that it was raining. He was charged with energy and he left the window and finished putting on his clothes. Earlier that morning, when he had waked up for the first time, he had felt as if he were about to be caught by a complete consumption in his chest; it had seemed to be growing hollow all night and yawning underneath him, and he had kept hearing his coughs as if they came from a distance. After a while he had been sucked down into a strengthless sleep, but he had waked up with this plan, and with the energy to carry it out right away.

He snatched his duffel bag from under the table and began plunging his extra belongings into it. He didn't have much and a quarter of what he had was already in. His hand managed the packing so that it never touched the Bible that had sat like a rock in the bottom of the bag for the last few years, but as he rooted out a place for his second shoes, his fingers clutched around a small oblong object and he pulled it out. It was the case with his mother's glasses in it. He had forgotten that he had a pair of glasses.

He put them on and the wall that he was facing moved up closer and wavered. There was a small white-framed mirror hung on the back of the door and he made his way to it and looked at himself. His blurred face was dark with excitement and the lines in it were deep and crooked. The little silver-rimmed glasses gave him a look of deflected sharpness, as if they were hiding some dishonest plan that would show in his naked eyes. His fingers began to snap nervously and he forgot what he had been going to do. He saw his mother's face in his, looking at the face in the mirror. He moved back quickly and raised his hand to take off the glasses but the door opened and two more faces floated into his line of vision; one of them said, "Call me Momma now."

The smaller dark one, just under the other, only squinted as if it were trying to identify an old friend who was going to kill it.

Haze stood motionless with one hand still on the bow of the glasses and the other arrested in the air at the level of his chest; his head was thrust forward as if he had to use his whole face to see with. He was about four feet from them but they seemed just under his eyes.

"Ask your daddy yonder where he was running off to—sick as he is?" Sabbath said. "Ask him isn't he going to take you and me with him?"

The hand that had been arrested in the air moved forward and plucked at the squinting face but without touching it; it reached again, slowly, and plucked at nothing and then it lunged and snatched the shriveled body and threw it against the wall. The head popped and the trash inside sprayed out in a little cloud of dust.

"You've broken him!" Sabbath shouted, "and he was mine!"

Haze snatched the skin off the floor. He opened the outside door where the landlady thought there had once been a fire-escape, and flung out what he had in his hand. The rain blew in his face and he jumped back and stood, with a cautious look, as if he were bracing himself for a blow.

"You didn't have to throw him out," she yelled. "I might have fixed him!"

He moved up closer and hung out the door, staring into the gray blur around him. The rain fell on his hat with loud splatters as if it were falling on tin.

"I knew when I first seen you you were mean and evil," a furious voice behind him said. "I seen you wouldn't let nobody have nothing. I seen you were mean enough to slam a baby against a wall. I seen you wouldn't never have no fun or let anybody else because you didn't want nothing but Jesus!"

He turned and raised his arm in a vicious gesture, almost losing his balance in the door. Drops of rain water were splattered over the front of the glasses and on his red face and here and there they hung sparkling from the brim of his hat. "I don't want nothing but the truth!" he shouted, "and what you see is the truth and I've seen it!"

"Preacher talk," she said. "Where were you going to run off to?"

"I've seen the only truth there is!" he shouted.

"Where were you going to run off to?"

"To some other city," he said in a loud hoarse voice, "to preach the truth. The Church Without Christ! And I got a car to get there in, I got . . ." but he was stopped by a cough. It was not much of a cough—it sounded like a little yell for help at the bottom of a canyon—but the color and the expression drained out of his face until it was as straight and blank as the rain falling down behind him.

"And when were you going?" she asked.

"After I get some more sleep," he said, and pulled off the glasses and threw them out the door.

"You ain't going to get none," she said.

CHAPTER 12

In spite of himself, Enoch couldn't get over the expectation that the new jesus was going to do something for him in return for his services. This was the virtue of Hope, which was made up, in Enoch, of two parts suspicion and one part lust. It operated on him all the rest of the day after he left Sabbath Hawks. He had only a vague idea how he wanted to be rewarded, but he was not a boy without ambition: he wanted to become something. He wanted to better his condition until it was the best. He wanted to be THE young man of the future, like the ones in the insurance ads. He wanted, some day, to see a line of people waiting to shake his hand.

All afternoon, he fidgeted and fooled in his room, biting his nails and shredding what was left of the silk off the landlady's umbrella. Finally he denuded it entirely and broke off the spokes. What was left was a black stick with a sharp steel point at one end and a dog's head at the other. It might have been an instrument for some specialized kind of torture that had gone out of fashion. Enoch walked up and down his room with it under his arm and realized that it would distinguish him on the sidewalk.

About seven o'clock in the evening, he put on his coat and took the stick and headed for a little restaurant two blocks away. He had the sense that he was setting off to get some honor, but he was very nervous, as if he were afraid he might have to snatch it instead of receive it.

He never set out for anything without eating first. The restaurant was called the Paris Diner; it was a tunnel about six feet wide, located between a shoe shine parlor and a dry-cleaning establishment. Enoch slid in and climbed up on the far stool at the counter and said he would have a bowl of split-pea soup and a chocolate malted milkshake.

The waitress was a tall woman with a big yellow dental plate and the same color hair done up in a black hairnet. One hand never left her hip; she filled orders with the other one. Although Enoch came in every night, she had never learned to like him.

Instead of filling his order, she began to fry bacon; there was only one other customer in the place and he had finished his meal and was reading a newspaper; there was no one to eat the bacon but her. Enoch reached over the counter and prodded her hip with his stick. "Listenhere," he said, "I got to go. I'm in a hurry."

"Go then," she said. Her jaw began to work and she stared into the skillet with a fixed attention.

"Lemme just have a piece of theter cake yonder," he said, pointing to a half of pink and yellow cake on a round glass stand. "I think I got something to do. I got to be going. Set it up there next to him," he said, indicating the customer reading the newspaper. He slid over the stools and began reading the outside sheet of the man's paper.

The man lowered the paper and looked at him. Enoch smiled. The man raised the paper again. "Could I borrow some part of your paper that you ain't studying?" Enoch asked. The man lowered it again and stared at him; he had muddy unflinching eyes. He leafed deliberately through the paper and shook out the sheet with the comic strips and handed it to Enoch. It was Enoch's favorite part. He read it every evening like an office. While he ate the cake that the waitress had torpedoed down the counter at him, he read and felt himself surge with kindness and courage and strength.

When he finished one side, he turned the sheet over and began to scan the advertisements for movies, that filled the other side. His eye went over three columns without stopping; then it came to a box that advertised Gonga, Giant Jungle Monarch, and listed the theaters he would visit on his tour and the hours he would be at each one. In thirty minutes he would arrive at the Victory on 57th Street and that would be his last appearance in the city.

If anyone had watched Enoch read this, he would have seen a certain transformation in his countenance. It still shone with the inspiration he had absorbed from the comic strips, but something else had come over it: a look of awakening.

The waitress happened to turn around to see if he hadn't gone. "What's the matter with you?" she said. "Did you swallow a seed?"

"I know what I want," Enoch murmured.

"I know what I want too," she said with a dark look.

Enoch felt for his stick and laid his change on the counter. "I got to be going."

"Don't let me keep you," she said.

"You may not see me again," he said, "—the way I am."

"Any way I don't see you will be all right with me," she said.

Enoch left. It was a pleasant damp evening. The puddles on the sidewalk shone and the store windows were steamy and bright with junk. He disappeared down a side street and made his way rapidly along the darker passages of the city, pausing only once or twice at the end of an alley to dart a glance in each direction before he ran on. The Victory was a small theater, suited to the needs of the family, in one of the closer subdivisions; he passed through a succession of lighted areas and then on through more alleys and back streets until he came to the business section that surrounded it. Then he slowed up. He saw it about a block away, glittering in its darker setting. He didn't cross the street to the side it was on but kept on the far side, moving forward with his squint fixed on the glary spot. He stopped when he was directly across from it and hid himself in a narrow stair cavity that divided a building.

The truck that carried Gonga was parked across the street and the star was standing under the marquee, shaking hands with an elderly woman. She moved aside and a gentleman in a polo shirt stepped up and shook hands vigorously, like a sportsman. He was followed by a boy of about three who wore a tall Western hat that nearly covered his face; he had to be pushed ahead by the line. Enoch watched for some time, his face working with envy. The small boy was followed by a lady in shorts, she by an old man who tried to draw extra attention to himself by dancing up instead of walking in a dignified way. Enoch suddenly darted across the street and slipped noiselessly into the open back door of the truck.

The handshaking went on until the feature picture was ready to begin. Then the star got back in the van and the people filed into the theater. The driver and the man who was master of ceremonies climbed in the cab part and the truck rumbled off. It crossed the city rapidly and continued on the highway, going very fast.

There came from the van certain thumping noises, not those of the normal gorilla, but they were drowned out by the drone of the motor and the steady sound of wheels against the road. The night was pale and quiet, with nothing to stir it but an occasional complaint from a hoot owl and the distant muted jarring of a freight train. The truck sped on until it slowed for a crossing, and as the van rattled over the tracks, a figure slipped from the door and almost fell, and then limped hurriedly off toward the woods.

Once in the darkness of a pine thicket, he laid down a pointed stick he had been clutching and something bulky and loose that he had been carrying under his arm, and began to undress. He folded each garment neatly after he had taken it off and then stacked it on top of the last thing he had removed. When all his clothes were in the pile, he took up the stick and began making a hole in the ground with it.

The darkness of the pine grove was broken by paler moonlit spots that moved over him now and again and showed him to be Enoch. His natural appearance was marred by a gash that ran from the corner of his lip to his collarbone and by a lump under his eye that gave him a dulled insensitive look. Nothing could have been more deceptive for he was burning with the intensest kind of happiness.

He dug rapidly until he had made a trench about a foot long and a foot deep. Then he placed the stack of clothes in it and stood aside to rest a second. Burying his clothes was not a symbol to him of burying his former self; he only knew he wouldn't need them any more. As soon as he got his breath, he pushed the displaced dirt over the hole and stamped it down with his foot. He discovered while he did this that he still had his shoes on, and when he finished, he removed them and threw them from him. Then he picked up the loose bulky object and shook it vigorously.

In the uncertain light, one of his lean white legs could be seen to disappear and then the other, one arm and then the other: a black heavier shaggier figure replaced his. For an instant, it had two heads, one light and one dark, but after a second, it pulled the dark back head over the other and corrected this. It busied itself with certain hidden fastenings and what appeared to be minor adjustments of its hide.

For a time after this, it stood very still and didn't do anything. Then it began to growl and beat its chest; it jumped up and down and flung its arms and thrust its head forward. The growls were thin and uncertain at first but they grew louder after a second. They became low and poisonous, louder again, low and poisonous again; they stopped altogether. The figure extended its hand, clutched nothing, and shook its arm vigorously; it withdrew the arm, extended it again, clutched nothing, and shook. It repeated this four or five times. Then it picked up the pointed stick and placed it at a cocky angle under its arm and left the woods for the highway. No gorilla in existence, whether in the jungles of Africa or California, or in New York City in the finest apartment in the world, was happier at that moment than this one, whose god had finally rewarded it.

A man and woman sitting close together on a rock just off the highway were looking across an open stretch of valley at a view of the city in the distance and they didn't see the shaggy figure approaching. The smokestacks and square tops of buildings made a black uneven wall against the lighter sky and here and there a steeple cut a sharp wedge out of a cloud. The young man turned his neck just in time to see the gorilla standing a few feet away, hideous and black, with its hand extended. He eased his arm from around the woman and disappeared silently into the woods. She, as soon as she turned her eyes, fled screaming down the highway. The gorilla stood as though surprised and presently its arm fell to its side. It sat down on the rock where they had been sitting and stared over the valley at the uneven skyline of the city.

CHAPTER 13

On his second night out, working with his hired Prophet and the Holy Church of Christ Without Christ, Hoover Shoats made fifteen dollars and thirty-five cents clear. The Prophet got three dollars an evening for his services and the use of his car. His name was Solace Layfield; he had consumption and a wife and six children and being a Prophet was as much work as he wanted to do. It never occurred to him that it might be a dangerous job. The second night out, he failed to observe a high rat-colored car parked about a half-block away and a white face inside it, watching him with the kind of intensity that means something is going to happen no matter what is done to keep it from happening.

The face watched him for almost an hour while he performed on the nose of his car every time Hoover Shoats raised his hand with two fingers pointed. When the last showing of the movie was over and there were no more people to attract, Hoover paid him and the two of them got in his car and drove off. They drove about ten blocks to where Hoover lived; the car stopped and Hoover jumped out, calling, "See you tomorrow night, friend"; then he went inside a dark doorway and Solace Layfield drove on. A half-block behind him the other rat-colored car was following steadily. The driver was Hazel Motes.

Both cars increased their speed and in a few minutes they were heading rapidly toward the outskirts of town. The first car cut off onto a lonesome road where the trees were hung over with moss and the only light came like stiff antennae from the two cars. Haze gradually shortened the distance between them and then, grinding his motor suddenly, he shot ahead and rammed the back end of the other car. Both cars came to a stop.

Haze backed the Essex a little way down the road, while the other Prophet got out of his car and stood squinting in the glare from Haze's lights. After a second, he came up to the window of the Essex and looked in. There was no sound but from crickets and tree frogs. "What you want?" he said in a nervous voice. Haze didn't answer, he only looked at him, and in a second the man's jaw slackened and he seemed to perceive the resemblance in their clothes and possibly in their faces. "What you want?" he said in a higher voice. "I ain't done nothing to you."

Haze ground the motor of the Essex again and shot forward. This time he rammed the other car at such an angle that it rolled to the side of the road and over into the ditch.

The man got up off the ground where he had been thrown and ran back to the window of the Essex. He stood about four feet away, looking in.

"What you keep a thing like that on the road for?" Haze said.

"It ain't nothing wrong with that car," the man said. "Howcome you knockt it in the ditch?"

"Take off that hat," Haze said.

"Listenere," the man said, beginning to cough, "what you want? Quit just looking at me. Say what you want."

"You ain't true," Haze said. "What do you get up on top of a car and say you don't believe in what you do believe in for?"

"Whatsit to you?" the man wheezed. "Whatsit to you what I do?"

"What do you do it for?" Haze said. "That's what I asked you."

"A man has to look out for hisself," the other Prophet said.

"You ain't true," Haze said. "You believe in Jesus."

"Whatsit to you?" the man said. "What you knockt my car off the road for?"

"Take off that hat and that suit," Haze said.

"Listenere," the man said, "I ain't trying to mock you. He bought me thisyer suit. I thrown my othern away."

Haze reached out and brushed the man's white hat off. "And take off that suit," he said.

The man began to sidle off, out into the middle of the road.

"Take off that suit," Haze shouted and started the car forward after him. Solace began to lope down the road, taking off his coat as he went. "Take it all off," Haze yelled, with his face close to the windshield.

The Prophet began to run in earnest. He tore off his shirt and unbuckled his belt and ran out of his trousers. He began grabbing for his feet as if he would take off his shoes too, but before he could get at them, the Essex knocked him flat and ran over him. Haze drove about twenty feet and stopped the car and then began to back it. He backed it over the body and then stopped and got out. The Essex stood half over the other Prophet as if it were pleased to guard what it had finally brought down. The man didn't look so much like Haze, lying on the ground on his face without his hat or suit on. A lot of blood was coming out of him and forming a puddle around his head. He was motionless all but for one finger that moved up and down in front of his face as if he were marking time with it. Haze poked his toe in his side and he wheezed for a second and then was quiet. "Two things I can't stand," Haze said, "—a man that ain't true and one that mocks what is. You shouldn't ever have tampered with me if you didn't want what you got."

The man was trying to say something but he was only wheezing. Haze squatted down by his face to listen. "Give my mother a lot of trouble," he said through a kind of bubbling in his throat. "Never giver no rest. Stole theter car. Never told the truth to my daddy or give Henry what, never give him . . ."

"You shut up," Haze said, leaning his head closer to hear the confession.

"Told where his still was and got five dollars for it," the man gasped.

"You shut up now," Haze said.

"Jesus . . ." the man said.

"Shut up like I told you to now," Haze said.

"Jesus hep me," the man wheezed.

Haze gave him a hard slap on the back and he was quiet. He leaned down to hear if he was going to say anything else but he wasn't breathing any more. Haze turned around and examined the front of the Essex to see if there had been any damage done to it. The bumper had a few splurts of blood on it but that was all. Before he turned around and drove back to town, he wiped them off with a rag.

Early the next morning he got out of the back of the car and drove to a filling station to get the Essex filled up and checked for his trip. He hadn't gone back to his room but had spent the night parked in an alley, not sleeping but thinking about the life he was going to begin, preaching the Church Without Christ in the new city.

At the filling station a sleepy-looking white boy came out to wait on him and he said he wanted the tank filled up, the oil and water checked, and the tires tested for air, that he was going on a long trip. The boy asked him where he was going and he told him to another city. The boy asked him if he was going that far in this car here and he said yes he was. He tapped the boy on the front of his shirt. He said nobody with a good car needed to worry about anything, and he asked the boy if he understood that. The boy said yes he did, that that was his opinion too. Haze introduced himself and said that he was a preacher for the Church Without Christ and that he preached every night on the nose of this very car here. He explained that he was going to another city to preach. The boy filled up the gas tank and checked the water and oil and tested the tires, and while he was working, Haze followed him around, telling him what it was right to believe. He said it was not right to believe anything you couldn't see or hold in your hands or test with your teeth. He said he had only a few days ago believed in blasphemy as the way to salvation, but that you couldn't even believe in that because then you were believing in something to blaspheme. As for the Jesus who was reported to have been born at Bethlehem and crucified on Calvary for man's sins, Haze said, He was too foul a notion for a sane person to carry in his head, and he picked up the boy's water bucket and bammed it on the concrete pavement to emphasize what he was saying. He began to curse and blaspheme Jesus in a quiet intense way but with such conviction that the boy paused from his work to listen. When he had finished checking the Essex, he said that there was a leak in the gas tank and two in the radiator and that the rear tire would probably last twenty miles if he went slow.

"Listen," Haze said, "this car is just beginning its life. A lightening bolt couldn't stop it!"

"It ain't any use to put water in it," the boy said, "because it won't hold it."

"You put it in just the same," Haze said, and he stood there and watched while the boy put it in. Then he got a road map from him and drove off, leaving little bead-chains of water and oil and gas on the road.

He drove very fast out onto the highway, but once he had gone a few miles, he had the sense that he was not gaining ground. Shacks and filling stations and road camps and 666 signs passed him, and deserted barns with CCC snuff ads peeling across them, even a sign that said, "Jesus Died for YOU," which he saw and deliberately did not read. He had the sense that the road was really slipping back under him. He had known all along that there was no more country but he didn't know that there was not another city.

He had not gone five miles on the highway before he heard a siren behind him. He looked around and saw a black patrol car coming up. It drove alongside him and the patrolman in it motioned for him to pull over to the edge of the road. The patrolman had a red pleasant face and eyes the color of clear fresh ice.

"I wasn't speeding," Haze said.

"No," the patrolman agreed, "you wasn't."

"I was on the right side of the road."

"Yes you was, that's right," the cop said.

"What you want with me?"

"I just don't like your face," the patrolman said. "Where's your license?"

"I don't like your face either," Haze said, "and I don't have a license."

"Well," the patrolman said in a kindly voice, "I don't reckon *you* need one."

"Well I ain't got one if I do," Haze said.

"Listen," the patrolman said, taking another tone, "would you mind driving your car up to the top of the next hill? I want you to see the view from up there, puttiest view you ever did see."

Haze shrugged but he started the car up. He didn't mind fighting the patrolman if that was what he wanted. He drove to the top of the hill, with the patrol car following close behind him. "Now you turn it facing the embankment," the patrolman called. "You'll be able to see better thataway." Haze turned it facing the embankment. "Now maybe you better had get out," the cop said. "I think you could see better if you was out."

Haze got out and glanced at the view. The embankment

dropped down for about thirty feet, sheer washed-out red clay, into a partly burnt pasture where there was one scrub cow lying near a puddle. Over in the middle distance there was a one-room shack with a buzzard standing hunch-shouldered on the roof.

The patrolman got behind the Essex and pushed it over the embankment and the cow stumbled up and galloped across the field and into the woods; the buzzard flapped off to a tree at the edge of the clearing. The car landed on its top, with the three wheels that stayed on, spinning. The motor bounced out and rolled some distance away and various odd pieces scattered this way and that.

"Them that don't have a car, don't need a license," the patrolman said, dusting his hands on his pants.

Haze stood for a few minutes, looking over at the scene. His face seemed to reflect the entire distance across the clearing and on beyond, the entire distance that extended from his eyes to the blank gray sky that went on, depth after depth, into space. His knees bent under him and he sat down on the edge of the embankment with his feet hanging over.

The patrolman stood staring at him. "Could I give you a lift to where you was going?" he asked.

After a minute he came a little closer and said, "Where was you going?"

He leaned on down with his hands on his knees and said in an anxious voice, "Was you going anywheres?"

"No," Haze said.

The patrolman squatted down and put his hand on Haze's shoulder. "You hadn't planned to go anywheres?" he asked anxiously.

Haze shook his head. His face didn't change and he didn't turn it toward the patrolman. It seemed to be concentrated on space.

The patrolman got up and went back to his car and stood at the door of it, staring at the back of Haze's hat and shoulder. Then he said, "Well, I'll be seeing you," and got in and drove off.

After a while Haze got up and started walking back to town. It took him three hours to get inside the city again. He stopped at a supply store and bought a tin bucket and a sack of quicklime and then he went on to where he lived, carrying these. When he reached the house, he stopped outside on the sidewalk and opened the sack of lime and poured the bucket half full of it. Then he went to a water spigot by the front steps and filled up the rest of the bucket with water and started up the steps. His landlady was sitting on the porch, rocking a cat. "What you going to do with that, Mr. Motes?" she asked.

"Blind myself," he said and went on in the house.

The landlady sat there for a while longer. She was not a woman who felt more violence in one word than in another; she took every word at its face value but all the faces were the same. Still, instead of blinding herself, if she had felt that bad, she would have killed herself and she wondered why anybody wouldn't do that. She would simply have put her head in an oven or maybe have given herself too many painless sleeping pills and that would have been that. Perhaps Mr. Motes was only being ugly, for what possible reason could a person have for wanting to destroy their sight? A woman like her, who was so clear-sighted, could never stand to be blind. If she had to be blind she would rather be dead. It occurred to her suddenly that when she was dead she would be blind too. She stared in front of her intensely, facing this for the first time. She recalled the phrase, "eternal death," that preachers used, but she cleared it out of her mind immediately, with no more change of expression than the cat. She was not religious or morbid, for which every day she thanked her stars. She would credit a person who had that streak with anything, though, and Mr. Motes had it or he wouldn't be a preacher. He might put lime in his eyes and she wouldn't doubt it a bit, because they were all, if the truth was only known, a little bit off in their heads. What possible reason could a sane person have for wanting to not enjoy himself any more?

She certainly couldn't say.

CHAPTER 14

But she kept it in mind because after he had done it, he continued to live in her house and every day the sight of him presented her with the question. She first told him he couldn't stay because he wouldn't wear dark glasses and she didn't like to look at the mess he had made in his eye sockets. At least she didn't think she did. If she didn't keep her mind going on something else when he was near her, she would find herself leaning forward, staring into his face as if she expected to see something she hadn't seen before. This irritated her with him and gave her the sense that he was cheating her in some secret way. He sat on her porch a good part of every afternoon, but sitting out there with him was like sitting by yourself; he didn't talk except when it suited him. You asked him a question in the morning and he might answer it in the afternoon, or he might never. He offered to pay her extra to let him keep his room because he knew his way in and out, and she decided to let him stay, at least until she found out how she was being cheated.

He got money from the government every month for something the war had done to his insides and so he was not obliged to work. The landlady had always been impressed with the ability to pay. When she found a stream of wealth, she followed it to its source and before long, it was not distinguishable from her own. She felt that the money she paid out in taxes returned to all the worthless pockets in the world, that the government not only sent it to foreign niggers and a-rabs, but wasted it at home on blind fools and on every idiot who could sign his name on a card. She felt justified in getting any of it back that she could. She felt justified in getting anything at all back that she could, money or anything else, as if she had once owned the earth and been dispossessed of it. She couldn't look at anything steadily without wanting it, and what provoked her most was the thought that there might be something valuable hidden near her, something she couldn't see.

To her, the blind man had the look of seeing something. His face had a peculiar pushing look, as if it were going forward after something it could just distinguish in the distance. Even when he was sitting motionless in a chair, his face had the look of straining toward something. But she knew he was totally blind. She had satisfied herself of that as soon as he took off the rag he used for a while as a bandage. She had got one long good look and it had been enough to tell her he had done what he'd said he was going to do. The other boarders, after he had taken off the rag, would pass him slowly in the hall, tiptoeing, and looking as long as they could, but now they didn't pay any attention to him; some of the new ones didn't know he had done it himself. The Hawks girl had spread it over the house as soon as it happened. She had watched him do it and then she had run to every room, yelling what he had done, and all the boarders had come running. That girl was a harpy if one ever lived, the landlady felt. She had hung around pestering him for a few days and then she had gone on off; she said she hadn't counted on no honest-to-Jesus blind man and she was homesick for her papa; he had deserted her, gone off on a banana boat. The landlady hoped he was at the bottom of the salt sea; he had been a month behind in his rent. In two weeks, of course, she was back, ready to start pestering him again. She had the disposition of a yellow jacket and you could hear her a block away, shouting and screaming at him, and him never opening his mouth.

The landlady conducted an orderly house and she told him so. She told him that when the girl lived with him, he would have to pay double; she said there were things she didn't mind and things she did. She left him to draw his own conclusions about what she meant by that, but she waited, with her arms folded, until he had drawn them. He didn't say anything, he only counted out three more dollars and handed them to her. "That girl, Mr. Motes," she said, "is only after your money."

"If that was what she wanted she could have it," he said. "I'd pay her to stay away."

The thought that her tax money would go to support such trash was more than the landlady could bear. "Don't do that," she said quickly. "She's got no right to it." The next day she called the Welfare people and made arrangements to have the girl sent to a detention home; she was eligible.

She was curious to know how much he got every month from the government and with that set of eyes removed, she felt at liberty to find out. She steamed open the government envelope as soon as she found it in the mailbox the next time; in a few days she felt obliged to raise his rent. He had made arrangements with her to give him his meals and as the price of food went up, she was obliged to raise his board also; but she didn't get rid of the feeling that she was being cheated. Why had he destroyed his eyes and saved himself unless he had some plan, unless he saw something that he couldn't get without being blind to everything else? She meant to find out everything she could about him.

"Where were your people from, Mr. Motes?" she asked

him one afternoon when they were sitting on the porch. "I don't suppose they're alive?"

She supposed she might suppose what she pleased; he didn't disturb his doing nothing to answer her. "None of my people's alive either," she said. "All Mr. Flood's people's alive but him." She was a Mrs. Flood. "They all come here when they want a hand-out," she said, "but Mr. Flood had money. He died in the crack-up of an airplane."

After a while he said, "My people are all dead."

"Mr. Flood," she said, "died in the crack-up of an airplane."

She began to enjoy sitting on the porch with him, but she could never tell if he knew she was there or not. Even when he answered her, she couldn't tell if he knew it was she. She herself. Mrs. Flood, the landlady. Not just anybody. They would sit, he only sit, and she sit rocking, for half an afternoon and not two words seemed to pass between them, though she might talk at length. If she didn't talk and keep her mind going, she would find herself sitting forward in her chair, looking at him with her mouth not closed. Anyone who saw her from the sidewalk would think she was being courted by a corpse.

She observed his habits carefully. He didn't eat much or seem to mind anything she gave him. If she had been blind, she would have sat by the radio all day, eating cake and ice cream, and soaking her feet. He ate anything and never knew the difference. He kept getting thinner and

221

his cough deepened and he developed a limp. During the first cold months, he took the virus, but he walked out every day in spite of that. He walked about half of each day. He got up early in the morning and walked in his room—she could hear him below in hers, up and down, up and down—and then he went out and walked before breakfast and after breakfast, he went out again and walked until midday. He knew the four or five blocks around the house and he didn't go any farther than those. He could have kept on one for all she saw. He could have stayed in his room, in one spot, moving his feet up and down. He could have been dead and get all he got out of life but the exercise. He might as well be one of them monks, she thought, he might as well be in a monkery. She didn't understand it. She didn't like the thought that something was being put over her head. She liked the clear light of day. She liked to see things.

She could not make up her mind what would be inside his head and what out. She thought of her own head as a switchbox where she controlled from; but with him, she could only imagine the outside in, the whole black world in his head and his head bigger than the world, his head big enough to include the sky and planets and whatever was or had been or would be. How would he know if time was going backwards or forwards or if he was going with it? She imagined it was like you were walking in a tunnel and all you could see was a pin point of light. She had to imagine the pin point of light; she couldn't think of it at all without that. She saw it as some kind of a star, like the star on Christmas cards. She saw him going backwards to Bethlehem and she had to laugh.

She thought it would be a good thing if he had something to do with his hands, something to bring him out of himself and get him in connection with the real world again. She was certain he was out of connection with it; she was not certain at times that he even knew she existed. She suggested he get himself a guitar and learn to strum it; she had a picture of them sitting on the porch in the evening and him strumming it. She had bought two rubber plants to make where they sat more private from the street, and she thought that the sound of him strumming it from behind the rubber plant would take away the dead look he had. She suggested it but he never answered the suggestion.

After he paid his room and board every month, he had a good third of the government check left but that she could see, he never spent any money. He didn't use tobacco or drink whisky; there was nothing for him to do with all that money but lose it, since there was only himself. She thought of benefits that might accrue to his widow should he leave one. She had seen money drop out of his pocket and him not bother to reach down and feel for it. One day when she was cleaning his room, she found four dollar bills and some change in his trash can. He came in about that time from one of his walks. "Mr. Motes," she said, "here's a dollar bill and some change in this waste basket. You know where your waste basket is. How did you make that mistake?"

"It was left over," he said. "I didn't need it."

She dropped onto his straight chair. "Do you throw it away every month?" she asked after a time.

"Only when it's left over," he said.

"The poor and needy," she muttered. "The poor and needy. Don't you ever think about the poor and needy? If you don't want that money somebody else might."

"You can have it," he said.

"Mr. Motes," she said coldly, "I'm not charity yet!" She realized now that he was a mad man and that he ought to be under the control of a sensible person

The landlady was past her middle years and her plate was too large but she had long race-horse legs and a nose that had been called Grecian by one boarder. She wore her hair clustered like grapes on her brow and over each ear and in the middle behind, but none of these advantages were any use to her in attracting his attention. She saw that the only way was to be interested in what he was interested in. "Mr. Motes," she said one afternoon when they were sitting on the porch, "why don't you preach any more? Being blind wouldn't be a hinderance. People would like to go see a blind preacher. It would be something different." She was used to going on without an answer. "You could get you one of those seeing dogs," she said, "and he and you could get up a good crowd. People'll always go to see a dog.

"For myself," she continued, "I don't have that streak. I believe that what's right today is wrong tomorrow and that the time to enjoy yourself is now so long as you let others do the same. I'm as good, Mr. Motes," she said, "not believing in Jesus as a many a one that does."

"You're better," he said, leaning forward suddenly. "If you believed in Jesus, you wouldn't be so good."

He had never paid her a compliment before! "Why Mr. Motes," she said, "I expect you're a fine preacher! You certainly ought to start it again. It would give you something to do. As it is, you don't have anything to do but walk. Why don't you start preaching again?"

"I can't preach any more," he muttered.

"Why?"

"I don't have time," he said, and got up and walked off the porch as if she had reminded him of some urgent business. He walked as if his feet hurt him but he had to go on.

Some time later she discovered why he limped. She was cleaning his room and happened to knock over his extra pair of shoes. She picked them up and looked into them as if she thought she might find something hidden there. The bottoms of them were lined with gravel and broken glass and pieces of small stone. She spilled this out and sifted it through her fingers, looking for a glitter that might mean something valuable, but she saw that what she had in her hand was trash that anybody could pick up in the alley. She stood for some time, holding the shoes, and finally she put them back under the cot. In a few days she examined them again and they were lined with fresh rocks. Who's he doing this for? she asked herself. What's he getting out of doing it? Every now and then she would have an intimation of something hidden near her but out of her reach. "Mr. Motes," she said that day, when he was in her kitchen eating his dinner, "what do you walk on rocks for?"

"To pay," he said in a harsh voice.

"Pay for what?"

"It don't make any difference for what," he said. "I'm paying."

"But what have you got to show that you're paying for?" she persisted.

"Mind your business," he said rudely. "You can't see."

The landlady continued to chew very slowly. "Do you think, Mr. Motes," she said hoarsely, "that when you're dead, you're blind?"

"I hope so," he said after a minute.

"Why?" she asked, staring at him.

After a while he said, "If there's no bottom in your eyes, they hold more."

The landlady stared for a long time, seeing nothing at all.

She began to fasten all her attention on him, to the neglect of other things. She began to follow him in his walks, meeting him accidentally and accompanying him. He didn't seem to know she was there, except occasionally when he would slap at his face as if her voice bothered him, like the singing of a mosquito. He had a deep wheezing cough and she began to badger him about his health. "There's no one," she would say, "to look after you but me, Mr. Motes. No one that has your interest at heart but me. Nobody would care if I didn't." She began to make him tasty dishes and carry them to his room. He would eat what she brought, immediately, with a wry face, and hand back the plate without thanking her, as if all his attention were directed elsewhere and this was an interruption he had to suffer. One morning he told her abruptly that he was going to get his food somewhere else, and named the place, a diner around the corner, run by a foreigner. "And you'll rue the day!" she said. "You'll pick up an infection. No sane person eats there. A dark and filthy place. Encrusted! It's you that can't see, Mr. Motes.

"Crazy fool," she muttered when he had walked off. "Wait till winter comes. Where will you eat when winter comes, when the first wind blows the virus into you?"

She didn't have to wait long. He caught influenza before winter and for a while he was too weak to walk out and she had the satisfaction of bringing his meals to his room. She came earlier than usual one morning and found him asleep, breathing heavily. The old shirt he wore to sleep in was open down the front and showed three strands of barbed wire, wrapped around his chest. She retreated backwards to the door and then she dropped the tray. "Mr. Motes," she said in a thick voice, "what do you do these things for? It's not natural."

He pulled himself up.

"What's that wire around you for? It's not natural," she repeated.

After a second he began to button the shirt. "It's natural," he said.

"Well, it's not normal. It's like one of them gory stories, it's something that people have quit doing—like boiling in oil or being a saint or walling up cats," she said. "There's no reason for it. People have quit doing it."

"They ain't quit doing it as long as I'm doing it," he said.

"People have quit doing it," she repeated. "What do you do it for?"

"I'm not clean," he said.

She stood staring at him, unmindful of the broken dishes at her feet. "I know it," she said after a minute, "you got blood on that night shirt and on the bed. You ought to get you a washwoman . . ."

"That's not the kind of clean," he said.

"There's only one kind of clean, Mr. Motes," she muttered. She looked down and observed the dishes he had made her break and the mess she would have to get up and she left for the hall closet and returned in a minute with the dust pan and broom. "It's easier to bleed than sweat, Mr. Motes," she said in the voice of High Sarcasm. "You must believe in Jesus or you wouldn't do these foolish things. You must have been lying to me when you named your fine church. I wouldn't be surprised if you weren't some kind of a agent of the pope or got some connection with something funny."

"I ain't treatin' with you," he said and lay back down, coughing.

"You got nobody to take care of you but me," she reminded him.

Her first plan had been to marry him and then have him committed to the state institution for the insane, but gradually her plan had become to marry him and keep him. Watching his face had become a habit with her; she wanted to penetrate the darkness behind it and see for herself what was there. She had the sense that she had tarried long enough and that she must get him now while he was weak, or not at all. He was so weak from the influenza that he tottered when he walked; winter had already begun and the wind slashed at the house from every angle, making a sound like sharp knives swirling in the air.

"Nobody in their right mind would like to be out on a day like this," she said, putting her head suddenly into his room in the middle of the morning on one of the coldest days of the year. "Do you hear that wind, Mr. Motes? It's fortunate for you that you have this warm place to be and someone to take care of you." She made her voice more than usually soft. "Every blind and sick man is not so fortunate," she said, "as to have somebody that cares about him." She came in and sat down on the straight chair that was just at the door. She sat on the edge of it, leaning forward with her legs apart and her hands braced on her knees. "Let me tell you, Mr. Motes," she said, "few men are as fortunate as you but I can't keep climbing these stairs. It wears me out. I've been thinking what we could do about it."

He had been lying motionless on the bed but he sat up suddenly as if he were listening, almost as if he had been alarmed by the tone of her voice. "I know you wouldn't want to give up your room here," she said, and waited for the effect of this. He turned his face toward her; she could tell she had his attention. "I know you like it here and wouldn't want to leave and you're a sick man and need somebody to take care of you as well as being blind," she said and found herself breathless and her heart beginning to flutter. He reached to the foot of the bed and felt for his clothes that were rolled up there. He began to put them on hurriedly over his night shirt. "I been thinking how we could arrange it so you would have a home and somebody to take care of you and I wouldn't have to climb these stairs, what you dressing for today, Mr. Motes? You don't want to go out in this weather.

"I been thinking," she went on, watching him as he went on with what he was doing, "and I see there's only one thing for you and me to do. Get married. I wouldn't do it under any ordinary condition but I would do it for a blind man and a sick one. If we don't help each other, Mr. Motes, there's nobody to help us," she said. "Nobody. The world is a empty place."

The suit that had been glare-blue when it was bought was a softer shade now. The panama hat was wheat-colored. He kept it on the floor by his shoes when he was not wearing it. He reached for it and put it on and then he began to put on his shoes that were still lined with rocks.

"Nobody ought to be without a place of their own to be," she said, "and I'm willing to give you a home here with me, a place where you can always stay, Mr. Motes, and never worry yourself about."

His cane was on the floor near where his shoes had been. He felt for it and then stood up and began to walk slowly toward her. "I got a place for you in my heart, Mr. Motes," she said and felt it shaking like a bird cage; she didn't know whether he was coming toward her to embrace her or not. He passed her, expressionless, out the door and into the hall. "Mr. Motes!" she said, turning sharply in the chair, "I can't allow you to stay here under no other circumstances. I can't climb these stairs. I don't want a thing," she said, "but to help you. You don't have anybody to look after you but me. Nobody to care if you live or die but me! No other place to be but mine!"

He was feeling for the first step with his cane.

"Or were you planning to find you another rooming house?" she asked in a voice getting higher. "Maybe you were planning to go to some other city!"

"That's not where I'm going," he said. "There's no other house nor no other city."

"There's nothing, Mr. Motes," she said, "and time goes forward, it don't go backward and unless you take what's offered you, you'll find yourself out in the cold pitch black and just how far do you think you'll get?"

He felt for each step with his cane before he put his foot on it. When he reached the bottom, she called down to him. "You needn't to return to a place you don't value, Mr. Motes. The door won't be open to you. You can come back and get your belongings and then go on to wherever you think you're going." She stood at the top of the stairs for a long time. "He'll be back," she muttered. "Let the wind cut into him a little."

That night a driving icy rain came up and lying in her bed, awake at midnight, Mrs. Flood, the landlady, began to weep. She wanted to run out into the rain and cold and hunt him and find him huddled in some half-sheltered place and bring him back and say, Mr. Motes, Mr. Motes, you can stay here forever, or the two of us will go where you're going, the two of us will go. She had had a hard life, without pain and without pleasure, and she thought that now that she was coming to the last part of it, she deserved a friend. If she was going to be blind when she was dead, who better to guide her than a blind man? Who better to lead the blind than the blind, who knew what it was like?

As soon as it was daylight, she went out in the rain and searched the five or six blocks he knew and went from door to door, asking for him, but no one had seen him. She came back and called the police and described him and asked for him to be picked up and brought back to her to pay his rent. She waited all day for them to bring him in the squad car, or for him to come back of his own accord, but he didn't come. The rain and wind continued and she thought he was probably drowned in some alley by now. She paced up and down in her room, walking faster and faster, thinking of his eyes without any bottom in them and of the blindness of death.

Two days later, two young policemen cruising in a squad car found him lying in a drainage ditch near an abandoned construction project. The driver drew the squad car up to the edge of the ditch and looked into it for some time. "Ain't we been looking for a blind one?" he asked.

The other consulted a pad. "Blind and got on a blue suit and ain't paid his rent," he said.

"Yonder he is," the first one said, and pointed into the ditch. The other moved up closer and looked out of the window too.

"His suit ain't blue," he said.

"Yes it is blue," the first one said. "Quit pushing up so close to me. Get out and I'll show you it's blue." They got out and walked around the car and squatted down on the edge of the ditch. They both had on tall new boots and new policemen's clothes; they both had yellow hair with sideburns, and they were both fat, but one was much fatter than the other.

"It might have uster been blue," the fatter one admitted.

"You reckon he's daid?" the first one asked.

"Ast him," the other said.

"No, he ain't daid. He's moving."

"Maybe he's just unconscious," the fatter one said, taking out his new billy. They watched him for a few seconds. His hand was moving along the edge of the ditch as if it were hunting something to grip. He asked them in a hoarse whisper where he was and if it was day or night.

"It's day," the thinner one said, looking at the sky. "We got to take you back to pay your rent."

"I want to go on where I'm going," the blind man said.

234

"You got to pay your rent first," the policeman said. "Ever' bit of it!"

The other, perceiving that he was conscious, hit him over the head with his new billy. "We don't want to have no trouble with him," he said. "You take his feet."

He died in the squad car but they didn't notice and took him on to the landlady's. She had them put him on her bed and when she had pushed them out the door, she locked it behind them and drew up a straight chair and sat down close to his face where she could talk to him. "Well, Mr. Motes," she said, "I see you've come home!"

His face was stern and tranquil. "I knew you'd come back," she said. "And I've been waiting for you. And you needn't to pay any more rent but have it free here, any way you like, upstairs or down. Just however you want it and with me to wait on you, or if you want to go on somewhere, we'll both go."

She had never observed his face more composed and she grabbed his hand and held it to her heart. It was resistless and dry. The outline of a skull was plain under his skin and the deep burned eye sockets seemed to lead into the dark tunnel where he had disappeared. She leaned closer and closer to his face, looking deep into them, trying to see how she had been cheated or what had cheated her, but she couldn't see anything. She shut her eyes and saw the pin point of light but so far away that she could not hold it

235

[handwritten marginalia:]

weird that she doesn't care about Enoch's dead body

he's finally not antsy, it took death

too late now, he's gone to the afterlife

emphasis on seeing

these words remind me of bones

reminds me of the first description of Haze

another call to the first description of Haze

interesting that the word "he" is used when connected to disappeared

more mention of sight/eyes, also light vs dark

thinks Haze or something about him cheated her?

steady in her mind. She felt as if <u>she were blocked at the</u>
<u>entrance of something.</u> She sat staring with <u>her eyes shut,</u>
<u>into his eyes,</u> and felt as if she had finally got to the be-
ginning <u>of something she couldn't begin,</u> and she saw him
moving farther and farther away, farther and farther into
the darkness <u>until he was the pin point of light.</u>